Our House

Our House
Barbara König

Translated by Roslyn Theobald
in collaboration with the author

Northwestern University Press
EVANSTON, ILLINOIS

Hydra Books
Northwestern University Press
Evanston, Illinois 60208-4210

Originally published in German under the title *Personenperson* in 1965 by Carl Hanser Verlag, Munich. Copyright © 1965 by Carl Hanser Verlag. English translation copyright © 1998 by Northwestern University Press. Published 1998 by Hydra Books/Northwestern University Press. All rights reserved.

Printed in the United States of America

ISBN 0-8101-1512-3

Library of Congress Cataloging-in-Publication Data

König, Barbara, 1925–
     [Personenperson. English]
     Our house / Barbara König ; translated by Roslyn Theobald in collaboration with the author.
          p. cm.
     "Hydra books"—T.p. verso.
     ISBN 0-8101-1512-3 (alk. paper)
     I. Theobald, Roslyn. II. Title.
PT2671.O23P413 1998
833'.914—dc21   97-47238
                                                        CIP

Every one of us is his own small society.
                                        Novalis

We might have guessed: This will lead to trouble. It isn't the first time, either. Each of us has put every one of us in danger at one time or another, and some of us more than once. There are differences of course, and one danger is not like every other; now, this afternoon, as we watch Nadine, our suspicions growing, it seems to us that there is only one threat: Love. Compared with love, even Cyril's obsessiveness and Anatol's death études are nothing but harmless idiosyncrasies—we can deal with these things, we can put up a fight, but what is happening to Nadine is beyond our control: whoever falls in love surrenders the fortress.

The way she's walking down the street! With a rain hat as broad as a wagon wheel, with a bundle of roses on her arm and a spirited stride that would be a puzzle to us if the answer weren't at her side: the man who animates her steps, and whom she has known for only a few hours—the man of her future, as she hopes, and we all fear.

We don't look at him. Maybe he's tall, maybe he's blond; we don't want to know. Because that's our only chance: that he remain in the shadows.

It is cool and yet already warm, a mongrel of a season; even this is dangerous: late post-winter, early pre-spring, uncertainty, stirring hope . . . The world seems to be playing along: puddles in every gutter, heaven in every puddle, a blue tiger-striped street. It's in the air, and a little boy is whistling, *taralimpida-taralimpida*, of love. The forces are against us.

They're talking, not to say anything really, but to hear each other's voices, they can't get enough of each others' voices; not yet. Nadine laughs. How extraordinary her presence, now, here! No wonder she's forgotten us, we could almost forget ourselves, especially now, saying good-bye at the front door. We need all of our strength just to stay who we are, and we already regret it: we all want to be Nadine, which is to say, we would be a whole, which is to say, we would simply not exist at all. Obliviousness is our best state.

Nadine is fumbling around in her handbag for her keys; her companion is smiling. The brim of her hat makes it impossible for him to kiss her, so he simply lays his hand on her cheek. But we know immediately that this hand is better than a kiss: a nest, a pillow; a place to stay. The moment expands, moist, sparkling, tiger-striped.

"Ah," says Nadine.

Our door is heavy, it has a knob in the shape of a hunting horn, weights impede its closing and prolong the good-bye. Through this hesitantly shrinking space Nadine discerns the remnants of the moment: the face, the silhouette, the raised hand, the street in which puddles are fading away.

We're in no hurry.

We are all happily settled in, no one has any reason to flee from this house. No one even has that option.

Cyril writes these reports, in part from his own impulse, in part at our behest (it's the only way we can find out what's happening in our house), and in part because one of us has to earn a living. He has a hard time of it. The editor, a man named Stranitzky, who takes Cyril's articles and pays a decidedly modest compensation in return, especially given that, to use Agatha's words, our heart's blood courses through them, this editor can't stand the plural.

"If you would only let me use the singular," Cyril says, "everything would simply flow from that; no aggravation, no complications . . . " But we just laugh at the thought: we tried that once, we won't do it again. That was when Cyril pretended to be all of us, and there was no end of complaints. Whoever left the house had to expect to be taken for Cyril; most of us didn't like that at all, if only because the majority of us are women, and we simply had no way to defend ourselves. To this day there are people who are convinced that Cyril is the only person living in our house, a thought that only Vladimir finds amusing; the rest of us are exasperated.

"Even duality would work," Cyril says, and this is a compromise we find downright shameful: If we are ready to admit that a person is not a singular entity but has at least one other self, a doppelgänger, as it were—why not admit the whole truth? What happened to all the others we once were, from childhood on, let alone the ones we hide so successfully, until one day they turn up in the wrong place causing us embarrassment and making us think? They are there, and it is false and unwise to deny them; it just isn't realistic.

Cyril gave in; basically all he cares about is his work. As long as he is allowed to write, he'll do anything. The very fact that he has come up with this explanation shows how obliging he is: he talks about himself in the third person, and he never makes any pretenses. Of course, he knows how exacting we are: No article leaves the house unedited, every one of us has to read it before it goes out. We aspire to relative objectivity, assuming there is such a thing, or at least the broadest possible subjectivity. If any one of us comes off looking too good, we delete; we're very sensitive about things like that.

Now that Nadine is bringing us this new experience, an experience we never asked for, Cyril is the one most affected. He knows what it means: he won't be able to work in peace anymore; our house, which has been quiet for some time, will become a meeting place for a most extraordinary cast of characters, Cyril will have to mention all of them in his story. Stranitzky will howl.

"What?" he asked this morning, grabbing what is left of his

hair. "You don't know how many of you there are? Somewhere between five and fifteen, you say? You're asking for trouble." Cyril insisted on the facts: that we don't know to this day how large our house actually is; that new characters keep showing up from time to time while others disappear into their rooms without in fact leaving.

"No one leaves here for good," Cyril said. "We all stay, until."

Stranitzky, a man somewhat like Anatol, except that he knows how to turn the productions of his mind into concrete achievements, didn't want to hear about all this. He shook his head, causing his neck bones to crack, a sign of his gentle character and the fact that he seldom says no.

"Please don't get me wrong," he said, "but the idea is abstruse: a dozen people in one person! No one is going to believe you. They've never been able to come up with more than a simple split, *Alas you know, two souls reside . . .* "

"So, it's just the number that bothers you?"

Stranitzky's neck bones cracked again; he quieted them and said:

"I can't really form a rational opinion. The artist in me says yes, the businessman says no, the critic doesn't like it either . . . "

"And what does the editor say?" Cyril asked.

The editor kept quiet and then nodded, silently, which again speaks for him. Cyril had won, the first round at any rate.

Nadine, in the hallway, has laid her handbag and gloves on the chest of drawers, and now she's carefully removing her hat and setting it down next to them; only then does she take off her coat. She has already freed one arm and is making a quarter-turn in order to grab the collar, when she hears Cyril say:

"Of all things. Just what we need." Nadine gives a start; for a moment the coat hangs from her right shoulder, the hem brushing the floor. Then she gathers it up without saying a word, slips out of the second arm, and chooses a hanger—cheerfully, unconcerned, as if she hadn't heard a thing. She picks up her handbag and gloves and goes into the living room.

Dombrowskaya is sitting at her table next to the patio doors playing solitaire. She looks up and says, a nine of hearts in her raised hand:

"So it is true. An encounter." She lets the card fall to the table and begins preparing her cigarette holder, two hand-widths of ebony and two finger-widths of amber.

"Yes," Nadine says, "yes."

"You're forgetting that you're not alone," Dombrowskaya says.

"I *was* alone," says Nadine. She folds her arms, lets her head fall back, and says "I." She draws out the vowel until it sounds like *aye*, "aye, aye," and we know it would be useless to interrupt her: after five, six repetitions the word loses its meaning, and what's left is a helpless diphthong, melded vowels, grotesque and a bit embarassing.

"I?" she asks again, already uncertain.

"There, you see," says Dombrowskaya, "no one has been able to keep it up for very long."

We don't use the word *traitor*, we're all too familiar with the I-attempt. We have each tried it at one time or another, and each of us has succeeded for some number of seconds, never longer, and we have all tried, like Nadine, to hold onto that moment. We would be perfectly irresistible, or so we believe, each of us, if only we were alone. Cyril is certain that we are standing between him and fame; he forgets that he limits us as well. No one of us can achieve greatness as long as the others are there, and most of us have learned to accept this fact. We prefer diversity to what would be, of necessity, a one-sided eminence.

"What would we be without our doubts," says Dombrowskaya, "without our many voices? In our house," she says, "everyone counts. We are facets in the eye of a fly; wherever anyone is missing a blind spot appears.

"If only we hadn't been through all this before," she says to Nadine. "Are you going to keep doing the same things over and over again?" This is typical of Dombrowskaya: she is no longer interested in novelty, it bores her a little. "Once you've had your eyes open for a couple of decades you will have seen what's possible. The rest will be repetition." She smiles; she finds it quite amusing.

Dombrowskaya, we always tell ourselves, enhances the value of our house. She bestows an air of relaxed serenity on the place and spares us the trouble of constant redecorating on the inside and an expensive paint job on the outside.

Here Bozena makes her entrance. We're like a tourist hotel at the beginning of the season, one guest after the other. Cyril, sitting at his desk, keeps getting more and more churlish.

"That's what we get. We let you out and then the crowd shows up." He points to the chairs around him: they are all occupied, Vladimir is lying on the rug, and Penny has set herself up under the table as if in a doghouse. "There's hardly a place to put your foot down," he says.

"Go ahead, count," Dombrowskaya says. Cyril gets to eight. "That's not so bad," she says, "we've had more." This is the moment Agatha arrives.

"Of course," says Dombrowskaya.

"Nine," says Cyril.

"Ten would be worse." We think she's referring to Sandra.

"It had to be now," says Cyril, "just when I'm in the middle of my work." He grabs a bundle of notes and shakes them bitterly. "If things keep on like this nothing will ever get done."

"Better just to leave things be," says Dombrowskaya, and she's not referring to Cyril. Nadine straightens her shoulders and says:

"I don't know what you're talking about."

Without moving her head, she lets her eyes wander observantly, "like a visitor to a zoo who has mistakenly found herself in the middle of an open-air habitat," says Vladimir, already planning a charming little story. "Stay calm," he says, "no sudden movement! The beasts are unpredictable."

"The problem is," says Anatol, "that she can't behave any other way. It's the way she communicates." These words arouse Penny's curiosity, the dear child wants to know what's going on.

"Has she started something? What is she up to?" Vladimir laughs.

"Nadine," explains Bozena, "was accompanied to the door by a new acquaintance, the new acquaintance laid his hand on Nadine's cheek, Nadine said 'ah' . . . That's all."

"What?" cries Penny. "That's all there is to it? Nothing more?"

"The brat is never satisfied," says Vladimir, but no one laughs. It's this "ah" that gave us a start; we recognize the tone, it was a welcome to something wondrous, which is always something dangerous, too. Nadine has exposed us, from now on anything is possible.

In the meantime, she works an old ploy to make this man attractive to us; she compares him to the three men who were most important to us in our past: Viola, Dombrowsky, and Jeremy. To use Agatha's words, they were the men we loved.

"He is as handsome as Viola," she says, "but in a different way." Out of the corners of her eyes she sees how Kay jumps. "As impish as Jeremy" (this is meant for Bozena) "and certainly as passionate . . . " Sandra can't be persuaded, she believes her own eyes, and nothing else. "A man like Dombrowsky," Nadine says, and Penny's ears perk up.

"A man like every other man," says Cyril.

"A troublemaker," says Anatol.

"You have no idea," says Nadine.

But unfortunately we have, we see the dangers: assuming we all become *I*. What then? We'll make this stranger a present of ourselves, a reward so to speak, and whether or not he really does see this gift as a reward will not depend on us. What if he just accepts us with a polite thanks and then casually sets us aside? Or even worse: he carefully looks us over, dismantles us, lays us out in separate parts, and then complains that we're not of one piece like some cast-iron chair. Anyway, Anatol asks, why go to all the trouble of becoming an I if you can't think of anything better to do than give it away?

7

Nadine mimes concurrence.

"Yes, yes," she says, "you're all very right." But as she goes to the windows to draw the curtains, because it's finally getting dark, she sees the sky between the houses and the branches, an opalescent puddle reflecting a not yet awakened earth, and says:

"It will never be so very spring again."

"Spring," says Cyril, "is not an adjective," and with that the opportunity to win Nadine over has been lost, our fears remain unresolved, nothing has been decided.

"If I'm to make anything of this affair, it will have to continue. But if it does continue I won't be able to make anything of it, because I won't be able to work."

"You can take notes and keep them for later, when you've got more time," says Nadine, who'll use any means to subvert our opposition. But now the others are protesting. Agatha appears and in a choked voice expounds on our feelings and on the marketplace where Cyril intends to profit from them, thus infuriating Cyril, because the idea isn't his, but Nadine's. And even while he's defending himself he's interrupted by Kay, who, unrestrained and with gloomy mien, accuses Cyril of having destroyed one of her last ideals, thus provoking Vladimir to probe for the rest. "Am I one of them?" he asks coyly, at which point Kay turns and leaves the room with a resounding slam of the door; only Penny is delighted.

"Nothing against feelings for sale," says Dombrowskaya, "especially if you are already involved in commerce, or consumption. If, however, you not only put off but actively obstruct wage-earning year in and year out, and then suddenly decide to make money, exploiting, of all things, these more delicate experiences, then," she says, opening the palms of her hands to Cyril, as if demanding an explanation, "this hardly seems plausible."

Cyril is so hurt that he doesn't even respond, and we'll have to admit Dombrowskaya has been unfair: after all, it's not his fault that he works so little, it's ours.

"We can't accuse him of laziness," now even Bozena

observes. That's true. In his working phases we hear the drum of his keyboard all day long, hour after hour, his face grim from exertion, and we know that he would dearly love to send us all away, but this is precisely what we won't allow; we make our presence felt. At first we content ourselves merely by forcing him to call our existence to mind: we are here, we are here! When Cyril sullenly takes his fingers off the keys, we move on to suggestions like: Why don't we take a little walk, it's a shame to stay inside on such a beautiful day . . . All this stale air is going to age us, all this strain is going to make us ugly . . . We've been invited out for coffee . . . We have to make a phone call . . . And so on. Cyril puts up a heroic fight, but it's hopeless, there are too many of us.

When he finally gives in he staggers a little; he'll need an entire day to recover, we know that, perhaps an entire week, and maybe, this is what we're really hoping, he may even be finished for the whole season. Sometimes we're right. And for months we see his tormented face in the corridors, a reproach that touches but does not change us. Every day he goes without working makes him a little paler. And all the while we're trying to makes things as easy for him as we can. With truly generous compassion we disregard his steadily decreasing income; we begin to celebrate the simple life. At meals we indulge ourselves in a profusion of compliments: truly an excellent variety of potato, Nadine remarks, and Agatha expounds on the value of yogurt for beautiful skin. Dombrowskaya has fewer heart palpitations now that she drinks less coffee, as has Anatol since he stopped smoking so much. Bozena goes on in great detail regarding the healing power of her herb teas, which are at last being drunk . . . As if in a fairy tale we are all stunningly united, and for only one purpose, to encourage Cyril in his idleness.

Finally he's had enough; with one determined gesture he shatters our every effort: "Money! This isn't about money! It's about not being able to get rid of it!"

Respectful silence. We know this trait that's been part of

him since birth: that he has to unload whatever he has taken on. For a long time we tried to cure him of it, out of pity, and because we wanted to escape his compulsion. "I collect things too," Anatol said, "but I'm satisfied to lie here on the sofa. Why bother all those people out there? It's unproductive, and what's more, it's risky: if you're unlucky in your efforts, they'll jump all over you." Vladimir is even less sympathetic; only with great difficulty can he imagine that someone would rather work than play. But Cyril just shakes his head at all this, bitter, hurt. Nothing can help him. Dombrowskaya has recognized the injustice she did him and takes back her reproach.

Nadine responds to the seasons, a situation that forces us to keep an eye on the calendar. Spring, as trite as this may sound, is suspect to begin with, but even transitions have their dangers; worst are the anticipated phases: a spring day in winter, a summer day in spring, an autumn day in summer . . . And hoarfrost. When Nadine is in love, says Vladimir, then we always have hoarfrost: nothing is ordinary any longer, no post and no wire. Every haystack looks like a castle.

A day like today, for example, nothing but foreboding from morning on. And haven't we been proven right? We have.

"Think about it," says Dombrowskaya, "this isn't the first time you've gotten into mischief in such eerie weather. The day when Jeremy became so important . . . "

"I didn't have anything to do with that," says Nadine. "That was Bozena's doing. To me he was nothing more than a nice friend."

She's right. If it had been up to Nadine, Jeremy would be nothing more than a friend of the family, even today. Still, she is the one who gave Bozena her chance.

That was a day in March, corrupted by summery heat, a truly fateful day: streets lay deserted, the park was overflowing. Sparrows scuffled in puddles, children played, balls rolled, mothers took babies out for strolls, couples suffering from lack of space squeezed together, blackbirds chirped, pebbles crunched, the earth smelled like earth, an intrusive exhilaration sprouted, spit gushed from every bush, every bush promised blossoms, or greenery at the very least—anyone walking through the park on a day like this had only themselves to blame.

Nadine studied Jeremy's profile: an amusing profile. An amusing person. Red hair is attractive, especially because it's rarer in a man. What a pity, says Nadine, there's no way I can get involved with him; I need a man who can take care of me. I *have* a man who takes care of me.

They found an empty bench and sat down, because on such a day an empty bench seemed a treasure, at least a rarity, at least . . . Their lungs pumped hope; inhaled along with oxygen, it went straight for the red corpuscles, sent them loaded with so many parts per million on their way. They would have to have stopped breathing to evade hope. They would have to have evaded the season, the high-pressure front, the shared closeness.

"Damned spring," said Jeremy.

"I don't know," said Nadine.

She looked around and found the park appalling; Dombrowsky would laugh when she told him she had been sitting here on a bench. But she wouldn't tell him anything; since Menaggio she no longer talked much about herself. Dombrowsky considered this a good sign. He thought she had become more *substantial;* but she had simply become more remote. She didn't even want to talk to Jeremy: he appeared to be sufficiently occupied with himself. Nadine looked at her watch.

"I have to go home."

"Oh, really," said Jeremy. She heard disappointment in his words and she liked it.

Actually she had wanted to stand up: instead she remained sitting, leaning slightly forward, her head lowered, as if listening for something. Jeremy didn't say anything, but she saw his feet standing on the sandy path, in brown oxfords, and there was nothing distinctive about them, nothing at all.

Bozena looked down at Jeremy's shoes: these shoes brought tears to her eyes, although, or because, they were anything but pitiable, just the opposite. They were a medium brown, not very large for a man, fashionably narrow, impeccably polished and tied: shoes, thoughtfully selected and cared for, treated with respect, maybe even love . . . Shoes which had no other purpose than to cover the feet of a man who couldn't be held accountable for having feet, a man who was never even asked if he wanted to walk upon the earth on two feet, if he wanted to walk at all, at all upon this earth . . . It was the futility she sensed in the effort a man had expended on his shoes that made her cry.

"They're good shoes," said Jeremy, "they cost sixty-five marks, maybe only sixty. You should never believe me, I lie all the time." If this had been Nadine she would have understood immediately and countered: Now, too, I hope! But Bozena had no such means at hand; she became sad at the thought that a man was forced to lie all the time, and she asked herself why this might be. He must be desperate.

"You always lie?"

"Yes," said Jeremy, "but always in correspondence with the truth, in correspondence with *a* truth at any rate."

"Well then . . . "

Jeremy laughed, but that didn't fool her: she heard the dissonance in his voice, the hidden cry for help. She didn't believe his eyes either: they were of a very indistinct color and seemed never to know exactly what they were seeing.

"Shall we walk a bit!" Jeremy said, and Bozena kept hearing the words: the unifying *we* which had not existed a moment ago, the intimately peremptory imperative and the *walk* which pointed so confidently to the future, a future which apparently was already at hand.

"Yes, a bit," she repeated, attempting to downplay an event which had already taken place in its entirety and would not be diminished either through words or through deeds.

They walked. He wasn't much taller than she; he had red hair and the light shone through his ears.

He asked if they would see each other again; that was simple politeness: they had already progressed beyond the if-questions and now needed only to deal with when and where.

"If you'd like?" Bozena asked. This was also a mere formality. They made a date. Bozena looked at her watch.

"I have to get back," she said. She didn't say *back home.*

They ate fish at a restaurant on the edge of town. Jeremy waited, Bozena explored. Every question went unasked, the interlude was wondrous. She looked at him: he was still as light as a feather, at the slightest whiff of air from her he would float away, she would be able to catch him and lay him down on the table, admire him; but any tiny gust meant danger for him, an opening door, a diner sneezing at the next table . . . She had already decided to ask, to weigh him down with dates and details, and with worries . . . She was ready to take on the burden.

No, Jeremy was a stranger in town, even though he had been living here for some time, he was a stranger in every city, in every country, he said, suddenly beginning to speak with an accent she couldn't place. That's why he preferred living abroad, because there it was understood that he had to have an accent, in his native country he had to explain at length: that he grew up abroad, in Ireland, because one grandmother was Irish, in Austria, because one grandmother was Austrian, in France—he could see how eagerly she was listening, but he had to disappoint her: no, even Jeremy had only two grandmothers, like everyone else. Still there were four great-grandmothers, and all of them seemed to have had an affinity for foreign lands, they had all married abroad, again and again, until one hardly knew which country was foreign and which was native, thus his accent in every language, thus his life in hotels.

"But you don't have an accent, at least you didn't have one a while ago."

"What was a while ago?" Jeremy asked.

That's why he was still single, he said, so that the curse wouldn't be passed on; because in order to break the chain he'd have to find a woman from his own country, but when he thought about it, he concluded there was no one with whom he shared a native country; if he wanted to marry it would have to be a foreigner after all, so he decided to leave things be.

"In our case," he said as he touched her hand, which was lying next to the bread plate, "it's somewhat different, we are from the same country."

"I'm not free," said Bozena, and this was the moment she first remembered Nadine and, in the same thought, cursed her, because she had forced a life on Bozena that was only meant for Nadine and not for her. Still, she took back the curse at once: Nadine didn't know anything about her, she was guilty of nothing. Instead she cursed the fact that Jeremy was a man: she would have preferred a child, an old man, or even an animal—any living being, as long as it needed her help. Why wasn't Jeremy a child? That wouldn't have bothered Nadine. But he was a child. She also took back the second curse and undertook never to curse anything again, it didn't suit her.

"Oh," said Jeremy. It was Bozena who had become heavier; she had only said four words and then fallen to the ground like a rock; Jeremy could talk for hours without gaining so much as a gram. The feather remained a feather. Still, she trusted her feelings more than his lightheartedness: he was in pain, she heard him calling out.

"My profession," he said, "takes me everywhere I want to go, what I mean is, I take my profession with me. I occupy myself with fields of study that others busied themselves with so long ago that it's worth the effort to study them again." He waved a hand through the air. "Ideas, questions, dead ends, philosophy . . . "

"But they don't make you happy."

Jeremy didn't answer; turning inward he sat there, a man occupied with his own internal processes; the outside world had fallen away. Bozena waited. Finally he lifted his fork to his mouth and then set it back down on his plate, looked up and smiled sheepishly. "It was only a bone," he said.

By the end of their rendezvous Bozena had decided not to see Jeremy again. He walked with her to a taxi stand.

"I am afraid there is no way to help you," she said.

"No," he said, suddenly intense, "there's no way to help me." He stood there and forced her to look at him.

"I hadn't realized," she said, carefully trying to retain her cheerful tone, "you have freckles."

"Only when I'm pale," said Jeremy. He had just divulged as much as he would ever divulge, she could expect no more; she realized this as he spoke.

"Will you come?" Jeremy asked.

"Of course," she said.

Living in a hotel provided him access to scores of little stories with which, Bozena believed, he avoided personal relationships. Thus his fascination with the key rack:

"When the rack is empty the hotel is full; when the hotel is full the rack is empty—isn't that remarkable?" And he told her about an *experience* that had upset him a great deal: Late one evening he returns to the hotel, greets the desk clerk, who is resting his hands on the counter and staring into empty space; the clerk turns around to get the key from the rack, but all of a sudden the number isn't there anymore, number sixteen comes right after number fourteen, the clerk is getting agitated, looks to the right, looks to the left, looks one row up, number fifteen is nowhere to be found; the clerk tries to explain the situation to himself and to Jeremy, to defend the hotel: In his many years at the hotel nothing like this has ever happened before and it was therefore impossible to hold the hotel responsible, who could prove to him that there had ever been a number fifteen, perhaps he, the guest, had just invented it, and the next thing you know, shouts the clerk, emboldened, a gentleman will come through the door and demand key number umpteen, right, number umpteen, and you see sir, even you are laughing, but the clerk, ever at the service of his guests, he will look for number umpteen, up and down, in every row . . . But I've been staying here for more than half a year, Jeremy interrupts, you know me after all . . . Know? shouts the clerk, my dear sir! I know this establishment and nothing else . . . He starts defending the hotel again, he's perturbed, gesticulating . . . Finally Jeremy goes out the door and into the street, and throwing back his head he attempts to decipher the illuminated script over the entrance, while the realization grows within him that this isn't his hotel after all, and for this reason there can be no key number fifteen . . .

"And then?" Bozena asked, "what did you do then?"

"Me? Nothing, of course. Is it always necessary to do something? I went to sleep."

"Yes, but—"

"In any case," said Jeremy, "you now know my room number, and please be so kind as to remember it."

Another time the elevator seems to have frightened him.

"It is the only object which sinks up," he said, "just imagine that: a cage which sighs and sinks up! And I always get stuck in contraptions like this, always. My head on the second floor, my feet still on the first. The only choice I have is either of seeing myself as a monkey in a cage or a prisoner behind bars. It takes me a long time to decide. Eventually, I make the part on the second floor a monkey and the part on the first floor a prisoner. I wait. I yell. Finally a chambermaid, her arms full of dirty linen, her brain full of cruelty and superstition, approaches along the corridor, and, seeing me, she believes that what she sees is a disembodied head lying here on the floor, and this doesn't bother her at all; on the contrary, she slinks closer, full of curiosity, but when she sees that it has red hair, she's terrified, spits three times out of the side of her mouth past the pile of laundry—why so careful, I ask myself, when it's going to be washed anyway, so she's stupid, too—she runs back down the entire length of the corridor, away. I sigh, and the elevator seems to take this as a signal, it sighs back and begins to sink, down this time. But there below—and this gives the story a rather nasty twist—is a furious guest in the lobby, he hisses at me, how dare I hold up the elevator for so long, he wishes there were five of him so he could give me the lynching I deserve, he gets in and rises unimpeded, I see by the arrow, up to the fourth floor. So, you see, in order to avoid all this abominable hassle, I never even considered moving into the main building, but went straight to the garden house: it doesn't have an elevator. You go directly up the stairway on the right, on past the second floor, up to the third, and there you'll find two doors, one is labeled 'bath' and the other 'fifteen.' That's where I live."

Bozena sighed.

"You don't have anything else to tell me?"

"I do," said Jeremy. "You are sweet and beautiful, if you'll allow me this pleonasm."

They met only during the day. In the evenings Bozena had to go, as she said, she never said *go home*. When she talked about her life *there*, then it was only superficially: I have to go away for two days, but I'll be back on Friday . . . On Friday he asked her how the trip had been. Oh, always the same, she replied, visits and dinner with friends, more obligation than pleasure. I'm not very much involved.

They had developed a system for making themselves inconspicuous, meeting in streets on the edge of town, in small cafés with wooden tables, beer gardens, coffee shops with stale pastries and secluded corners. Sometimes she arrived in Nadine's car, a little coupe with red upholstery.

"It's practical," said Jeremy, "but it doesn't suit you."

"Why should it?" said Bozena. They sat at a round table in a restaurant called Adler, or Schwarzer Adler.

"I can't really imagine," he said unexpectedly, "how you can have any life there at all. Too many contradictions . . . "

"It's not so bad," she said. "I keep things separate. As a matter of fact I don't actually live there; I only live with you."

A couple, tourists from America, joined them at their table even though the restaurant was almost completely empty. In their quest for the *real thing* they had discovered Adler, they ordered Rhine wine and wanted to make contact; the wife spoke German. To Bozena's amazement, Jeremy plunged right into the conversation, it seemed to Bozena to be a playful attempt at escape.

"The weather's been beautiful," the woman said, "we've been lucky, we've had beautiful weather everywhere, in Italy, Switzerland, and now here, too." Jeremy dissented immediately: How could anyone be so interested in the weather, something we had all experienced thousands of times, always in the same context, temperature, humidity, precipitation, clearing; approximately five kinds of snow, and just as many kinds of rain, and sunshine, of course, all this distributed over a minimal number of seasons . . . using up the capacity of one's senses on such meaningless features, to what end?

"What does he say?" the husband asked.

"He doesn't like weather."

"What weather?"

The woman turned back to Jeremy.

"But when you're on vacation good weather is important . . . "

Jeremy was not interested in compromises. Beautiful weather, bad weather, what kind of prejudices are these, weather is beautiful whenever it makes you feel good. Why don't you admit it: a delicate veil of mist over a valley—wouldn't it do you ten times as much good as some clear day of foehn in the mountains when the wind stings you with its needles the moment you crack open an eyelid.

"Yes, but the view . . . "

And hadn't such clarity always made them suffer, given them a kind of foehn-burn like patterns in a copper engraving or burn lines from too much sun, it was so numbing . . .

"What does he say?"

"I don't know," said the woman. Jeremy had one last argument:

"As long as you are walking in the fog no one can prove to you that you've lost your way, you can't even prove it to yourself. That's certainly worth something, isn't it?"

"But we don't like fog," she said.

"No, we don't," the husband said.

They parted smiling. The husband ordered a second bottle, in order to, as Jeremy observed while leaving, praise the advantages of weather in general, the advantages of clear weather in particular, while his fog cover grew.

Out in the street his expression suddenly turned dark, and when she raised her eyebrows in question, he turned on her:

"You're amusing yourself? You think I'm funny? I'm a jester, a comic?" His eyes were so fierce that she became frightened.

"Don't worry," she said, "nothing's going to happen to you."

"Sometimes," he said maliciously, "you talk to me as if I were a beggar: 'Wait here, no don't go away, come back, I have something for you . . . '" He stomped the ground with his foot like a spoiled child. "I can't take that, I won't play along."

"But you're wrong," said Bozena, fighting back the tears. "If anyone here is begging, it's me."

As they sat in the car, he leaned over to her and kissed her gently on the neck, below her ear. It was the first time, he had never kissed her before.

"You are good," he said, "not that there's anything you can do about it, but I thank you anyway." Immediately after that he acted as if nothing had happened and carried on about the potted palm in the lobby of his hotel.

"It is part of the staff and has very specific duties: to deny northern climes, and never to show signs of change; it may neither grow nor blossom; it's dusted every day, it has a right to be. Whenever it begins to look sickly it's brought to a gardener and another palm is put in its place, one exactly like it, so that no one notices the substitution. Where days are filled with departures and arrivals, the palm represents permanence . . . "

"And?"

"Ah," Jeremy cried, "you are waiting for the point of the story! I see I've spoiled you. But this time there isn't any point, it was an observation totally free of purpose, *l'art pour l'art*, so to speak . . . "

"You are wonderful," said Bozena.

"Well, then it had a point after all," said Jeremy.

Bozena was free for a couple of days, no one there, she said, they could even go out, preferably not to the theater, but maybe to the movies and later to a nightclub, if he'd like.

"I can't go out until after dark," Jeremy said. "Before that the magnolias in front of my window require my attention."

"Magnolias? Until now you've only mentioned chestnut trees."

"So you don't know? In every annual cycle of the chestnut tree there is a magnolia hour, one single hour when the buds have grown long but are still very pale, and then in the light of the evening sun—you see, it has to be the evening sun— for an hour they appear to be magnolias about to bloom. It is their costume ball, they look forward to it all winter long . . .

By morning everything will be unmasked, the pink dream gone, nothing left but poisonously green leaves pointing straight down . . . Are you interested?"

"That sounds awful."

"It only sounds that way," said Jeremy. "You see they're in complete agreement with this metamorphosis. It's a scene they've added so that they will be all the happier going back to being chestnut trees . . . "

"I don't know . . . "

"Of course you don't know, and that's what makes you different from a tree—trees always know."

"Good," she finally said, "I'll come. It's probably only going to happen once."

"That's more or less true," said Jeremy.

The figure of Bozena following this decision is a sight that can still make us laugh: she trembled.

"On the road to the gallows," says Cyril, "she sensed the end."

Then she asked for a cognac, something she almost never did, and while they were sitting in an unpleasant but out-of-the-way espresso bar, she drank not one but three. After the third glass, she announced:

"Now I know what it reminds me of."

"What reminds you?"

"This here, this café. It is like an operating theater: chrome and glass everywhere, and the instruments are being sterilized in the espresso machine." Jeremy took her glass and asked if she would like another little narcotic, and Bozena was hurt because this fearless Jeremy had begun to seem alien and not entirely sane.

"There you see her true requirements," says Anatol. "She's ready to make any sacrifice for a poor and tormented Jeremy, but as soon as he was feeling good the ground went out from under her feet, she got scared and headed for the nearest exit . . . That scene with the napkins . . . "

That's Vladimir's cue, no plea for mercy can keep him

from reveling in the comedy of the napkins, even Anatol laughs, Bozena is the only one who blushes when she sees herself again, sitting in the espresso bar, threatened by chrome and glass in the same way one might be threatened by knives, helplessly chilled, looking for a way out. It still isn't too late.

Just a little errand, she said to Jeremy, a dozen napkins to pick up at a shop where they do monograms. She'd like to have them today, she declares with unusual resolve, yes, definitely today.

They drive downtown. Jeremy waits in the car while Bozena goes into her linen shop. She almost runs, she's in a hurry to see her monogram again, like a person who has lost her memory, says Vladimir, and who believes it will all come back to her if she can only read her name . . .

Yes, the napkins are ready, finished two days ago, and the hand embroidery turned out wonderfully, madam must of course judge for herself. Bozena is satisfied; she carries each piece, individually, from the counter to the glass door and examines, enveloped in the respectful silence of the staff, a monogram that is not, and yet is, hers, Nadine's monogram. She mumbles niceties, *very skillfully done* and *flawless*, all the while attempting to talk herself into believing that these letters refer to her, and that she, accordingly, belongs in Dombrowsky's house, has obligations . . . She struggles to reach a decision.

Once it has been made, she forgoes the rest of the inspection and asks for the bill. As she leaves the store she looks for words to tell Jeremy, an excuse that won't hurt him: Please forgive me . . . and I know you'll think it's silly, but . . . She's certain the rest will come back to her once she gets to the car.

It doesn't work out that way. For unfortunately, Vladimir says, with an exaggerated expression of regret, it is just closing time for all the offices: too many people on the street, hundreds and hundreds . . . They go past the parked cars, stop, look at one another, look into the cars and go on . . .

Jeremy can't stand the proximity of so many living beings,

can't stand their stares. His head leaning sideways against the window, he is breathing onto the pane, turning it a cloudy white.

This image forces Bozena to capitulate. She laughs while reproaching herself: How could she have left him alone for so long, here in this swarm! She had only been thinking of herself. As if she were the one who mattered! He is the one who matters; Jeremy is lonesome, Jeremy is afraid.

She throws the napkins into the back seat. Jeremy turns his head toward her and says:

"The sun is about to set, it will be time for the magnolias."

"Yes," says Bozena, "it will be time."

She would have been able to get this far on her own, the way to the desk clerk who took key number fifteen down from the rack, on past the potted palm and the cagelike elevator, which at this very moment was sinking up with a sigh . . . She knew the garden stairway to the right, up to the third floor, the two doors, one of which was labeled fifteen.

She didn't recognize his room.

She immediately went to the window and saw that Jeremy had kept his word; it was the magnolia hour.

"Well, did I lie?"

"You lied when you said you always lied."

"Yes, then too," said Jeremy.

This hour had twenty minutes at most; the evening sun left the chestnut trees in Jeremy's courtyard, the unique moment had passed, Bozena was preparing to move. She found it difficult. With her back she attempted to feel her way into the alien room she would now have to face. Jeremy's alien room. She remembered his shoes on the ground in front of the bench, tried again to find redemption in this scene, and didn't find it.

"So there!" said Jeremy. The sun had set. Bozena turned toward him.

"I think," she said, as her eyes haltingly followed the rotation of her body, "I should not have come."

That was the end of this romance. What happened to Bozena after this compels us to smile in sympathy and shake our heads: she is so difficult to teach. She clung to Jeremy, even after he had become Sandra's; she simply didn't want to believe it.

Sometimes at night she thought she heard him scream and it woke her up. Then it would be a long time before she could fall back asleep, and she would invent new words for him, entire litanies of endearment and consolation. But with the morning she knew that she had been mistaken; Jeremy wasn't screaming, Jeremy was happy.

Sometime near the end of August she heard about his illness. She bought fruit juice and tea biscuits and went to his hotel. In the entry to the garden house she met the doctor.

"You are the woman taking care of him?"

"I—yes," Bozena said. The doctor pressed his business card into her hand.

"Please keep me informed. If his fever goes up we'll have to transfer him to the clinic."

She tiptoed into his room. Jeremy had turned his face to the wall and didn't seem to hear her. As she bent over him she saw the blank stare of his eyes from behind reddened lids; the skin over his cheekbones seemed translucent and unnaturally taut.

"Jeremy," Bozena said. His whole body jerked as if he had just been hit.

"Jeremy," she said again, imploring. This time he reacted, his lids fell shut, his nostrils spread, a dismissive expression appeared on his lips. Jeremy had retreated. Bozena had raised her hand to wipe the hair back off his forehead; she let it be.

At this moment Sandra returned. Bozena left without a sound.

One afternoon in October she saw him in a café sitting at a table under the arcade. He was paging through a book, but his face had an aloof expression, a kind of distractedness that frightened her. The book appeared to be there for the sole purpose of preserving Jeremy's state of absence. Even when she walked up and stood next to him he didn't notice her.

"For God's sake," said Bozena, "what's wrong with you?" He suddenly came to.

"Nothing," he said. "I'm reading, as you can see."

"But you look awful—aren't you feeling well?"

"On the contrary, I feel great." She even took his malicious smile to be a sign of his ill health.

"I've never seen you looking so pale."

"I fear," said Jeremy, "that's all in the eye of the beholder." She finally understood.

"You don't trust me, you're like an enemy."

"Now, really," said Jeremy.

"I'd better go." He didn't stop her. Once she had taken a few steps she turned around and saw him sitting in front of his book, composed and withdrawn, not only from her.

That was the beginning of her meandering marches through the city, the endless hours in the park where she discovered lost souls among the passersby, fish out of water not able to find their way back, each of them making one last attempt at accommodation before death. She didn't know what she was looking for, she only knew that it wasn't Jeremy, at most it might have been the earlier Jeremy, or some other living being like him in its neediness, maybe an animal, or an old man, a child.

That's where things stand; she's still searching, and she is convinced that if it weren't for us she would have found what she was looking for long ago. This may also help to explain her rare but fiery outbursts, which don't contradict her otherwise gentle disposition but seem to complement it. She grabs onto the edge of a table, which, in spite of its accepted function, takes on the appearance of a baby's chest, and she screams:

"You are killing me! You are taking my life! I should blast you all to hell, right now, or it will all be too late . . . " We know what she means, and that she would up and leave us for any piddling infant. Still we allow her her anger, we even respect it; she has more or less the status of a protected species. We content ourselves merely with circumventing the laws she obeys, but we don't dare oppose them.

There's only one way to appease her: we put things off. "Some other time," we say, and "It doesn't have to be this very moment." Bozena quiets down, and an eerie stillness settles in, "as if following a great loss," says Agatha, who will use whatever word comes to mind, as long as it expresses a strong feeling. She doesn't mean loss, she means resignation.

Bozena has settled down again, but we know that she will keep longing, day in and day out, for The One Thing. You might think she had finally had enough of it, but no, she won't give up. "Only death will cure her," says Cyril, but we don't dare see this as a consolation: her death will also be ours.

"Every encounter," says Dombrowskaya, "is a misunderstanding: the person one knows is never the same person one has encountered—the encounter has changed him." That sounds like one of her sayings, and Nadine shrugs her shoulders impatiently, but Cyril takes notes and wants details: Does that mean that a person can only encounter the right partner, but cannot keep him, because he has already become the wrong partner? Or the other way around: that you must encounter the wrong partner in order to find the right partner?

"One chance in a thousand," says Dombrowskaya. But isn't it possible to find the right person without transforming him?

"In that case you haven't really encountered him," says Dombrowskaya, and we suddenly understand what she means; we remember the Jeremy sitting on the bench, the Jeremy whose shoes Bozena found so pitiable, and we remember the Jeremy in the restaurant who would use any excuse to escape his rescuer, "even a bone stuck in his throat," said Dombrowskaya, "that belonged to him alone. Because this stupid Bozena had missed seeing the transformation; because she wanted to keep on saving him." Bozena still doesn't see.

"For me," she says, "he is still the Jeremy on the bench." At that, even Anatol laughs. Dombrowskaya is patient.

"If you once rescue someone from a burning house," she says, "you can't do it a second time. And it's wrong to treat him as if he were forever trapped in a burning house."

"Yes," says Bozena, "but isn't it burning all the time and everywhere!"

"So, now we understand each other, meaning that we understand why we don't understand each other."

"You say the most amazing things," says Bozena.

For a moment it seems as if she has given up without a fight, but then she surprises us with her protest.

"Nadine," she says, "had an encounter, but has anything changed?" She looks around. "If it has, I haven't noticed."

"Bravo!" Cyril shouts. "Finally a logical thought."

"Just a bit precipitous," says Dombrowskaya. "We will only be able to tell after the next rendezvous . . . "

"Tonight at eight," says Nadine.

"For heaven's sake," says Anatol, "and here come our anxieties, things are getting dangerous again." Only Dombrowskaya remains calm.

"If there is any justification at all for this commotion," she says, "it's the possibility of bringing a new person into our midst. Apart from that . . . " She shrugs her shoulders. Of course. We know her point of view. She sees every event in this house in terms of whether or not it will summon another person. The question as to the character of this person is the only angle that still piques her curiosity. "I would like to know who's going to show up, and when. All sorts of things may happen."

Even her practice of turning experience into aphorism arises mainly from the need to create order for *the next one*: whoever it may be should be able to tell at first sight what the situation has to offer and thereby spare everybody a great deal of unnecessary repetition . . .

This is Dombrowskaya's wish alone; we have nothing against repetition, as long as it's pleasant and harmonizes to some extent with that which we, according to interest and temperament, consider to be our lives.

"Pleasant or not," says Cyril, "as long as it's the right experience. In my case, for example . . . "

Thinking about Cyril is like paging through a stack of old newspapers published during the years after the war.

Cyril said to his landlady: "My dear Mrs. Mayer, of course I'm pale, that's because I am an addict; you can tell an addict by his complexion. Nevertheless, my addiction is an acceptable one, even in your demanding circles: work. I'm lucky: if my sin were drink, drugs, or gambling, you would have shown me the door a long time ago. However, since all I suffer from is work, you talk about the outdoors in the context of health and complexion, and ignore the fact that we're simply dealing with nuances, happenstance . . .

"You want me to lead a healthy life: a young person needs fresh air, exercise, a little dancing now and then. Dear Mrs. Mayer, I am not interested in any of that. Like everyone with an addiction, all I care about is my addiction. And because it manifests itself at night, I also love the night. You may praise morning all you want—I detest it. The onslaught of the day, the spurious revival, the illusion that you may prevail after all, fed on blood sugar and daybreak, will be sacrificed to the heat of midday, no later . . . What I know of the morning: the blurred, battered, squandered life on the streets that bubbles up, raises blisters, and slowly sinks back in the afternoon; by evening the surface is clear, and finally by midnight it settles . . . "

"You should become a poet," said Mrs. Mayer.

As she left the room Cryil went over to the mirror and rubbed his cheeks.

"Pale," he said, "pale, pale . . . "

When Cyril arrived at the newspaper office that afternoon he found a note on his desk with the name Paul Jakob, the address, and instructions: twenty-five lines. For a minute he stared at it angrily, as if it were a personal affront, then he reached for the phone and ordered a pool car.

"Have a bad breakfast or something?" asked the photographer, who had already been informed and was waiting for Cyril at the reception desk. "Too much petty bullshit?" Cyril didn't say a word.

Paul Jakob was lying on the fifth floor of an apartment complex in a double bed made of birch, amidst painful cleanliness. Except for a bandage over his left eyebrow, there was nothing to indicate that he had been in an accident.

"He was in shock for a while, that's all," his wife said, and energetically pulled up two chairs. "He needs a sedative to get to sleep." Paul Jakob spoke so quietly that Cyril had to move closer. So, from the beginning: He, Paul Jakob, a long-haul truck driver, forty-five years old, had an accident; he ran into a tree, suffered a slight concussion, a cut on the face, and was taken away in shock. When was this and where? The night of . . . to . . . , on a boulevard near Friedrichshain. Good. And the cause of the accident? He had been passed by a man on a motorcycle, that's it, it gave him such a start that he couldn't hold onto the steering wheel. Now, wait a minute! That's just the way it happened, because he was hauling a load of sheet metal, thin sheets with edges as sharp as razor blades, and because the sheets were loosely loaded, that is, not tied down tightly enough, well they *were*, it's just that they were so sharp that they cut through the cables, and because the motorcycle passed him at just that moment. What moment? Paul Jakob saw him approaching in his rearview mirror, very fast along a country road, without a light, it was still daytime . . . Was his headlight on? No, of course not, it was still daytime! So the accident didn't take place on the night of . . . to . . . after all, but in the afternoon? At about the same time in the afternoon as now, five-thirty. So, the motorcycle approached, and then he, Paul Jakob, saw a shadow like a piece of paper in his rearview mirror, and the man on the motorcycle disappeared under it, and then there was an awful noise, the way there is when a piece of sheet metal falls off a truck, a rolling, ringing rumble, and at the same moment the man on the motorcycle roars by straight on down the road, he, Jakob, wants to step on the brakes because of the sheet metal, it can't just be left there, but then he sees the man on the motorcycle, he doesn't have a head, because the sheet metal—the edges are as sharp as razor blades, said Paul Jakob, and to explain his weak nerves: he had seen so many accidents, dead of all kinds, that is bound to happen, but not one of them had ever kept right on driving . . .

The photographer took two pictures, both of Paul Jakob in bed with a bandage over his left eyebrow, with the empty gaze of an innocent victim who is attempting in vain to comprehend how this could possibly have happened to him.

Meanwhile, in the kitchen Cyril asked the wife for a glass of water. He drank it standing up, his hand resting on the faucet, his gaze directed at a calendar photo of a young woman picking poppies at the edge of a wheat field under a sky full of woolly clouds; it was titled *Summer Delight*. He set the glass down before the photographer had a chance to make any snide remarks.

They wished Mr. Jakob well and left.

Back in the office Cyril wrote out twenty-five lines, taking care to be as objective as possible. He tried to convince himself that it was just an insignificant little accident. One fatality, an almost painless death didn't mean much in the statistics that incorporate hundreds of such incidents every weekend. In spite of this, he still felt queasy when he took his article to the typesetting department later that night.

The typesetting department was the one place where Cyril felt at home. When he walked through the machine room he felt as if he were in the bowels of an ocean liner, isolated and yet protected, and for him the smell of printer's ink and paper represented the promise, renewed every day, of the only possible life he could live. The typesetters were his friends; they shared their schnapps with him, and he drank to prove that he wasn't a wimp; he laughed at their off-color jokes, and they always took good care of his stories, producing a clean piece of work. Cyril's passion was for the process, not for the news; setting errors were the only things that upset him, reversed lines, muddled headers. A flawless makeup was the only thing that brought him true joy.

He didn't feel well. At a window whose bars safeguarded a courtyard full of garbage, he composed the final titles, counted the letters, and handed the copy to the waiting typesetter.

"Is that all?" the typesetter asked.

"That's all," said Cyril. He saw what *all* was. Asleep at daybreak, still holding a book in his hand, shallow dozing through the sounds of the day, waking up around one, bath, clean clothes, there was half the afternoon to spend before work would finally begin again . . . Impatience. Already life outside his work was getting bleak, already he was addicted to the night shift, brush proofs, typesetters, news in reflected letters, headlines three columns double-bold Antiqua . . . And so on, until retirement, then death, without ever having understood one single story.

Cyril went to the typesetting table and stood for a long time in front of his page in whose symmetry he no longer delighted. He read easily; he guided the news, cleanly framed and titled, through his eyes on into his brain where it was suitably filed away: leaded stories in mirrored script that weighed down his head to the point where he was forced to pass them on; they slid down to his feet, out to his hands, into his stomach until all parts including the trunk were full; his skin was like parachute silk, thin but rugged, he could count on it.

In the meantime he read an article which he himself had edited that night: "Mysterious Nurse" (*Bureau Report*):

Dr. Wilfert, the veterinarian from Tiefenbach, had a bizarre experience last Tuesday evening when he was called to an outlying farm to assist a cow with calving . . . Cyril was compelled to go along; he was the veterinarian Dr. Wilfert and parked his car out on the road next to a pile of gravel which retreated into the night the moment the headlights were extinguished; he was the one who an hour and a half later left the rescued cow and thankful farmer at the barn and followed the beam of his flashlight through the orchard back out to the county road. The nurse was standing next to the pile of gravel and asked if he might give her a lift, *only as far as Tiefenbach*, she said, the gravel crunching under her feet. He, Wilfert-Cyril, willingly opened the door, helped the nurse along with her midwife's bag into the car, got in himself, and took a cigarette out of his pocket.

Now he's looking for matches, reaches into his left-hand pocket, then into the right—at that point a flame leaps up out of the nurse's cigarette lighter. For the length of time it takes him to inhale, the veterinarian stares at a masculine fist—hair on back of the fingers, a broad thumbnail. He has only the time it takes to inhale for contemplation, then he takes action, mechanically: he turns the ignition on, turns it off, turns it on again, swears at the spark plugs and the battery, he gets out, raises the hood, bends over the motor . . . Now he asks the nurse to help: he will turn the ignition on again, and would she be so kind as to hold a spark plug, which seems to be loose, in place. It's an amateurish plan, but a veterinarian, after all, is not a mechanic . . . The nurse does what she is asked, the motor is running, *good* shouts the veterinarian out of the car window, *and would you please close the hood!* He waits until the person is standing next to the car . . . The passenger door is still open, cigarette smoke is biting his eyes, but he had already shifted into gear, turned on the headlights, stepped on the gas . . . He doesn't even look into the rearview mirror, the only thing on his mind is escape.

I am thankful that I'm a veterinarian, he says fifteen minutes later at the police station in Tiefenbach. The night sergeant nods and with his two index fingers continues typing out the list of items in the midwife's bag: tools, two number plates, a large kitchen knife . . .

"Is something wrong?" the typesetter asked.

"There's a pick in here," Cyril said and pointed to a spot between two paragraphs, "otherwise everything's all right." He heard the sounds again, the stamping of the rotary machine, the ventilator, and voices from the next table:

"How am I supposed to make a page out of this crap? . . . Humankind seems to be made up entirely of tits and brains. Tits are cheap, and what's left? Brains. And most brains are just as cheap."

"You're so right, but what else can you do? Use the tried and true mix: a little nature, a little zoo, a little technology. It doesn't make you feel any better, does it?"

Cyril took the lone footstool and sat down on it, but soon transformed it into a paper stand and sat down on the windowsill instead. The filth in the courtyard, garbage and litter, rusty iron and paper, now seemed to him to be no more than the necessary output of a daily newspaper: yesterday's news. One day per event, nothing more; what counted was newsworthiness.

About two in the morning he finished work and left the building with Jost, the sports editor. The street was a large room illuminated in neon. They knew the few figures they encountered: the ones with black bow ties, the ones zigzagging down the street, the ones with hands in their pockets and heads leaning forward—waiters, drunkards, people in despair. All with their collars turned up for protection, and because they were lonely; it was the uniform of nighttime wanderers.

Cyril loved neon light. Day seemed dim to him when compared with this brilliance. He began to repeat the word *neon:* "Neon, neon, neon . . . " Even before they had crossed the street it had become a complaint: "Neo-ono ohno . . . "

"What's with you?" Jost asked.

A few of their colleagues had already gathered in the Alpha. Schmitt, who was covering the war-crimes trials, complained about the impossibility of communicating the facts:

"It all goes way beyond imagining. Who reads what he reads, anyway?"

"I do," said Cyril, "and I have done so for an hour."

"You say: he murdered thousands—and no one listens. You say 'thousands' and the shutters close—end of reception. That may be a kind of defense because we'd all go crazy otherwise, but . . . "

"A fine defense: the individual is safe and humanity goes to hell!"

"We should be able to come up with a system to break through this resistance . . . "

"Maybe we can catch them off guard."

"No, in that case a little guile would be better: force the reader to identify with the story before you tell him what's really going on. Like this: Dear reader, imagine yourself on a sunny summer day in Grunewald. You play Ping-Pong with your children; smell the Scotch fir, feel the sand beneath your feet, hear the balls click . . . The same sounds are coming from the house next door, they're playing Ping-Pong, too. The neighbor is a businessman like you, he too is successful, he too is enjoying this Sunday afternoon with his family . . . You are making plans for your vacation; unfortunately it will only be possible during the school holidays, but even this time your wife has found a quiet little place at the shore, she'll take this burden off your shoulders, you won't have to bother . . . And so on. Then dinner is ready, so the table on the terrace is set, the same thing is happening at the neighbor's house, you go into the house, you wash your hands, eat, go to bed, sleep . . . And are awakened. The doorbell. No, it's not a delivery boy with a telegram. You may take a toothbrush and a bar of soap with you. This will be your last trip in a limousine, dear reader, after this there will only be freight cars, and not even that for very long . . . And your family will have the same kind of journey, your wife, your children . . . And the neighbors? Where everything is just the same? No, not this neighbor, because, you see, he has a different name, Müller not Rosenbaum . . . "

Now Cyril could see how his coffee cup was beginning to melt away; even as he was stirring the coffee, the rim sank and spread out into the shape of a soup bowl, then a flat dinner plate, and finally soaking into the tablecloth on which a small brown pillar of coffee stood. He picked up the spoon and the handle dripped through his fingers.

"Try this," he said to Jost, and handed him the spoon. His colleagues looked at him, began talking to him, and about him:

"What in the world has gotten into you? Not all here, are we?"

"You're looking pretty pasty . . . "

"No wonder, in this light . . . "

"Neon," said Cyril, "nee, ohno, ohno . . . "

"Now it's really gotten to him," Schmitt said. The others tried to hide their discomfort in laughter. Cyril didn't pay them any attention: he had just discovered the motorcycle rider. He was standing behind the bar asking for silverware, Cyril watched him through a display case that contained apples and biscuits. The guy had no head.

Someone ordered a Steinhäger for Cyril, "before he falls off his chair." Mehnke, a member of the foreign affairs section, started a discourse on the dangers of the night shift:

"Very few can take it over the long haul, sooner or later they all crack. But once they get used to it none of them wants to give it up. Of course, for a guy like this," he said nodding his head toward Cyril, as if Cyril no longer heard anything, "it'll be pretty bad. He's still growing. We all keep growing until we're twenty-five."

"Leave him alone, he'll be all right. A good night's sleep, less coffee . . . "

"Now I remember: Helbig, the same thing happened to him. First he couldn't take looking at any more reports, and then . . . A nice little breakdown, that's the direction it's taking . . . "

Cyril saw the motorcycle rider coming out from behind the display case. He was carrying his head along with the schnapps.

"Well then, it can't have been all that bad," said Cyril. Now Schmitt and Jost were beginning to show their concern openly.

"I'll take him home," said Schmitt.

"Maybe we should drive by the hospital? I think he could use a doctor."

"Just like Helbig," said Mehnke. "First he reads what he reads, and then he hears voices that aren't there. Right?" he asked Cyril, and Cyril answered:

"The day is noisy."

Another group of newspaper people who had probably been hanging out in Wagner's Bar made a noisy entrance from the street. Cyril saw the neon room through the open door; it appeared blue and clean in contrast to the café, which was now filled to capacity with noise and smoke. Cyril grew sad as the door closed again.

For some time, with all the aversion he could muster, he faced down a goulash soup which had been forced on him, then he occupied himself with fighting off the tabletop which kept rising up at him; he bumped his glass. Jost, who no longer let him out of his sight, caught it as it fell.

"Check, please," shouted Schmitt.

Cyril found himself right in the middle of a moment, squeezed in between past and future, on the edge of a piece of sheet metal. He understood that this point could not provide adequate footing for his existence; he felt so thin that he couldn't confirm his reality even to himself: he simply wasn't. This thought was both comforting and discomforting: that it was comforting seemed to confirm its accuracy, that it was discomforting made him suspect he might be wrong. Nevertheless, he was able to leave this edge and move to another, to that part of the moment which was previously future and now had become present, while the preceding present became past, and only the already existent past remained past unchanged, so that he was now, as he determined with great interest, dealing with a moment that consisted of two pasts and one present, but no future. He also was able to get himself picked up by both arms and led away by Schmitt and Jost.

During his stay at the clinic Cyril was chiefly occupied with protecting himself from nurses, an activity made all the more demanding by the fact that he was surrounded by them day and night. At first the nurses could not understand his unusual conduct. One day he asked Theresa, the nurse responsible for his case, where she had left her handbag.

"Which bag do you mean?"

"You know, the big brown one with the handle!"

"I left that one at home," she said cheerfully, "because I have everything I need here at the station."

"I could have guessed that," Cyril said.

Another time he asked her, with feigned innocence, if she wasn't sorry that he had no car.

"Not at all! We're just as happy with you without a car!" This puzzled him somewhat.

"My bed doesn't have a number, does it?"

"No, but your room has one." She was remarkably open; she never seemed to deny anything.

"And if I wanted to smoke a cigarette now, would you light it for me?"

"I'm no fool," she said, "I'm strictly forbidden to do that."

He showed symptoms of paranoia:

"You can hide all sorts of things under an apron like that," he said. And: "It doesn't have to be such an enormous knife, a little one would do. Why even bother with a knife," he asked and watched thoughtfully as Theresa made his bed, "when poison is so much simpler . . . " For several days he had to be persuaded to take each bite.

It wasn't until he mentioned that it would never occur to him to become a veterinarian that they began to understand his affliction. The nursing supervisor had read the article and even remembered the details.

That afternoon Theresa brought her gloves in and asked him how he liked the color. Cyril was indifferent.

"I think," she said, "they look even smaller than they are because of the seam. Besides, I do have rather small hands, don't you agree?

"Yes, of course," said Cyril.

But it wasn't until she came back with his dinner that he first started to show signs of alertness.

"The gloves were very beautiful," he said. "Won't you show me your hand again? Really it is such a tiny hand!" He laughed. "No, we're so easily deceived!" From then on he improved.

The city they finally released him into was a model city under a glass plate, the edges of which captured the blue, a flawless horizon. It seemed to Cyril that he had never before seen such sharp contours. The buildings revealed a delicate geometry, the layout of the streets, a clarity that charmed him. Wherever he turned he found perfection, a design drafted with the finest possible point. As he walked he came to see the plan of a city in which living a happy life was virtually a commandment. He had forgotten the neon nights.

At the same time he became conscious of a state of extreme vulnerability; this, it seemed, was the price of his new vision, and it was not too high. He simply had to pay attention, be on guard! This was no longer a time for aimless wandering, from now on he would have to be alert: go around obstacles, avoid encounters, feel out dangers in advance— like a hemophiliac, he told himself, for whom any contact might be fatal.

It was five o'clock in the afternoon, and paying no heed to his warnings, his feet headed down the street to the newspaper building. The only concession he managed to wrest from them was a detour that spared him the front entrance; he wanted to take the back stairs.

Once he had come within fifty steps of the building he stopped and took it in: a walkway paved with gray stones running along an iron fence, imbedded in a knee-high footing, enclosing the parking lot; fire walls left and right covered with posters, a dog approaching him, a woman who walked past, and further away, advancing unremittingly, a streetsweeper. Behind the bars, in the courtyard, two rows of cars in spaces enclosed by chains and designated *reserved, reserved, reserved.* A man emerged from the back entrance, got into a delivery truck not parked in a reserved space; he tried several times to get the engine started; it produced a growling, futile noise.

The night shift had already begun; behind the second-floor windows florescent lights all went on at once; they flickered and seemed to be swallowing in eager anticipation. The tops of cars grasped for flashes of light. Cyril observed a hand wrapped around one of the squared-off bars, and saw that it was thin and the veins were blue. When the figure of a man appeared overhead and opened the window, he let go and stepped back. Even before the man had time to lean out and call to him, he was gone, past the streetsweeper, who was still approaching, but no longer in his direction. Tepid, milky patience flowed into him.

A bouquet of roses in a vase.

"This is getting serious," Cyril says.

Nadine is beaming; she cradles every single blossom in her hand and kisses it. Agatha hums: *Dark red roses for a lovely lady,* even though these roses are light-colored, salmon pink to medium red.

"Back then the roses were a lot like these," says Anatol.

Nadine cannot remember any other bouquet like this one, or maybe dozens of bouquets, and that she refuses to remember. But Dombrowskaya knows immediately what he means.

"This time we won't keep them; after they've wilted we'll throw them in the trash." But Anatol has already withdrawn.

Dombrowsky's last bouquet was there when we first moved in; Nadine, who can't remember it now, carried the flowers in herself and put them on the chest in the entryway. Even though the roses had long since gone bad, not simply wilted, but thoroughly rotted from the inside out. "Roses like black knots," said Anatol, "a mummy bouquet." He marred our move with images like that: "Don't you smell anything?" he asked each one of us in turn. "They stink. Decay, autumn, compost."

Fortunately no one had time to worry about Anatol's gloominess; nevertheless, the theme reappeared in Vladimir's work a short time later, in a sketch to be sure, which depicted Anatol as a doctor wearing glasses and a white coat. The scattered greenery displayed human characteristics, but none of us wanted to see ourselves in it and names were not named. Vladimir recited a text to go along with the sketch, and its prosody was so complicated that it made Penny pale with envy:

> In the waiting room
> Sat a sick potato;
> It had in its time
> Sprouted too frenzied
> And was now dying of cancer.
> The nearby radish
> From the drought most surely
> Was made bitter. This
> Frightened the cabbage, whose
> Inner decomposition was told in its leaves.
> To the left of a shriveled-up carrot
> An apple of the Morning Glow sort was hardly able to
> Resist its maggots.

The hygienically focused sun
Ate up off linoleum
Bacteria busily, while
The house Columnea Gloriosa
Maintained an arrogant silence:
It was sure of its health.

The magazine on the table
Praised Capri. It smelled
Like rotted roses, compost.

A spring in his step the doctor came.
His lens-aided eye
Read illness in Latin.
'Unfit for human consumption,'
So he spoke (in English, since he had once
A boy scout been). He quickly computed
The fees which escaped him,
But the Good Deed of the day
Had been due for decades, and so
Himself he overcame and called
By telephone, with a sonorous voice,
The city garbage collector.

It is diversions like this that upset our life. As much as we may hope to forget, there will always be one of us who will remember, at just the wrong time, and, seeing a bouquet of roses, will have to bring up compost.

"Ostentatious!" says Nadine. Vladimir's poetry doesn't amuse her at all. "And it's really so simple: where there are roses, there is love, and where there is love . . . " She looks around and asks, "What are you laughing about?" We are laughing. "You're just jealous," she says.

"I'll say," says Cyril, "we most certainly are. We'd all like to have such a bad memory." He mocks her: "It's really so simple: Where there are roses, there is love, and where there is love, there are no more questions. It seems to me it's quite the contrary . . . "

"I know what you mean," says Nadine. "Dombrowsky. But

that was an exception. Back then I didn't know that so many people could be hidden away in one person." At this we really start laughing.

"Do you know it now?" asks Cyril.

Nadine, back in Menaggio, had roses on her night table. She also had bottles of Asti, spumante and nonspumante. In addition to that, in front of her window, she had Lake Como, protected by an indescribably golden mist (indescribable for Cyril) from a sky which was entirely, and every bit as indescribably, October, nothing but October, an attack in blue.

Before this almost unbearable splendor, overcome again and again with a beauty which by this time must have seemed a burden, Nadine contemplated her experience with a new Dombrowksy in whom she would never have dared to believe: the gentle, rugged, gracefully self-assured, at the same time utterly infatuated, an extremely seductive Bel Ami. The engineer had been forgotten at the moment he was betrayed.

(In the meantime, the engineer was sitting a few hundred meters away in the lobby of another hotel across from a sheikh who had for this reason alone, and begging a thousand pardons, followed him into his vacation, because this was a unique, new, epoch-making project that could not be delayed . . . Engineer Dombrowsky had already decided. Used to determining the life of the private Dombrowskys unopposed, he swept aside the opposition of the newly awakened Bel Ami, the lover of his wife, whose demands, and that was his mistake, he counted among the projects that could be delayed.)

Nadine, surrounded by roses, spumante, much Lake Como, and even more October, in the classically peaceful pose of a woman who knows she is loved, is waiting for Romeo.

The man who returns is the engineer. A man under whose sober eyes the roses on the night table disintegrate into the most banal cliché in the language of flowers, compared with which even a cabbage would be capable of more expression—to whom the bottles standing on the night table bring no thoughts of intoxication, only of import duties; for whom the magic in front of the window flattens into a postcard vista, a cheap four-color print: red, gold, bright blue, and green . . .

"We're leaving," he says. "I'm sorry."

What happened after this, says Cyril, is something he will have to relate, because Nadine doesn't remember a thing, she only says it was such a shock, and carries on about despair and tears. Cyril, on the other hand, calls it an attack of hysteria and feels sorry for poor Dombrowsky. You have to see it through *his* eyes, he says, otherwise you can't get a clear picture. So, we make ourselves a picture, curious but reluctant, of Dombrowsky's travail: an unsuspecting man who returns to his hotel and announces to his wife that they have to interrupt their vacation, because he, unfortunately, for business reasons, must immediately . . . And who, instead of a rational answer, has a confession of adultery hurled his way, and how!

She doesn't state, as might be expected, staring coldly across the table: Dombrowsky, I have betrayed you, but you are the guilty one! (Or to put it another way: Darling, forgive me, I don't know how it could have happened, I only know that I'll never, ever again . . .) Not Nadine. Save me, she screams, they're chasing me, I can't get rid of them! He hadn't even taken off his coat. Hysteria, he thinks, she gets that from her mother, but who could have known that it would break out so soon . . . Right away, dear, he says, first let me get my coat off.

You've been away for such a long time, she sobs, much too long! (And he hardly has time to imagine what she means: but I've been here all the time, he says.) And they've got me in their claws, the cat, the angel, the glass . . . Who's got you in their claws? You have to save me, she howls, you're responsible . . . Not for everything, says Dombrowsky. For everything! screams Nadine.

At least he had gotten his coat off and was sitting down; he looked around mechanically at all of the things that had to be packed. Meanwhile, she continued to whine, more and more confused, it seemed to him: the tomcat was sitting in front of the door and had red eyes, that's right, everyone knows that in the night cats have green eyes, but this one had red eyes, and he didn't want to let her get by, or back either, so they stared at each other, but then a door opened and the tomcat ran away up the stairs, and she ran down the corridor to his room. Whose room? Room twenty-nine, said Nadine, it might have been twenty-six, it doesn't really matter, we're in twenty-six, said Dombrowsky, it doesn't matter, and that's where the angel was on the ceiling, a terrible angel with a sword in his hand, he said it was only the shadow of the drapes and the light from the pier—who said that? Twenty-nine, said Nadine, but it wasn't true, because how could the drapes get a hold of a sword?

Excuse me, Dombrowsky said at this point, stood up, and no longer thought about packing his suitcase, what were you doing in twenty-nine in the middle of the night, but then it couldn't have been in the middle of the night, because I was here all the time, but in the evening, what, I ask you . . . Nothing, said Nadine, and it wasn't even very far away, not even in the next building, not even on another floor, only a few steps, the same room, the same bed . . .

Adultery, said Dombrowsky and sat down again, so it's come to that. He tried to imagine that something dreadful had happened, but he couldn't make himself believe it, the hotel atmosphere seemed to resolve everything, exactly as Nadine had said, the same room, the same bed, the lake in front of the window . . . Twenty-nine or twenty-six, the difference was in a minor rotation . . . But you're supposed to help me, sobbed Nadine, don't you see how he's chasing me? He hasn't left me alone for one minute, since . . .

The angel or twenty-nine? asked Dombrowsky. He looked for a paradigm in his memory: A man in this situation, what does he feel? What does he do? He rants, he raves, he beats his wife, he gets up silently and goes to his lawyer, he buries his face in his hands and weeps . . . He didn't do any of these things, he just sat there, somewhat taken aback next to the table, and thought about how quickly everything had to be packed, and that he had to notify the desk clerk that they were leaving.

The angel, of course, cried Nadine, and the floor light . . . I thought, said Dombrowsky, it was the lantern on the pier. Yes no, yes no, she screamed, don't you understand? I ran away, and here at the door, here at the threshold, you know, the light in the floor with a thick pane of glass on top, it shines all night, all of a sudden there was a bang like an explosion, and it went pitch dark, I hardly touched it with the heel of my shoe, everyone's always walking over it, every one of them heavier than I am, but this time it shattered . . . And twenty-nine? Oh, twenty-nine, said Nadine and took what seemed to him her first real breath, it could be one hundred, it simply doesn't matter anymore . . .

Where is the angel now? asked Dombrowsky, and the tom-cat, and the glass? Are they in the room? Nadine opened her eyes wide: gone, she said, since you've been here they're gone. As they should be, said Dombrowsky, you've gotten rid of them and I've taken them on. He went to the closet, got his suitcase, and began packing his suits. It's too bad that I'm not affected by angels, and I hate cats, especially cats with red eyes, and glass is something I only appreciate in the form of glasses, and then only when they're filled with something high proof . . .

Monster, said Nadine. She wasn't whimpering anymore. That's all I wanted to know, she said, you don't love me. When a wife tells her husband that she has deceived him, and he acts as if nothing has happened, and even jokes about it . . . huh, she said, I thought so; I just wanted to be sure . . .

Suddenly, justifiably, Dombrowsky had enough; he slammed his suitcase shut and left the room without a word. In the corridor he met the tomcat; Dombrowsky went into a crouch and looked the startled animal in the eye: its eyes were neither red nor green, but yellow. Of course, it wasn't night but luminous day. He knocked on the door of room twenty-nine, curt but hard, and during the brief second he waited, potential faces of danger passed before his eyes, melding into the face of the seducer, the gentle, rugged, gracefully self-assured, at the same time utterly infatuated Bel Ami. And with him, the engineer Dombrowsky, who knew a lot about calculations but very little about himself, knew he could not compete.

The woman, who answered her door immediately, was sorry: for a week now she had been the only one staying in room twenty-nine, there was no man. He believed her (and also believed—after a glance into her greedy eyes—she was sorry). Nadine really had fantasized. To complete the picture, a confused-disturbed-angered Dombrowsky, having just decided not to allow this nonsense of his wife's to distract him from the demands of his business for one more minute, this Dombrowsky stumbled over the floor light, which had apparently been removed and covered in a makeshift fashion. For Dombrowsky, there remained a doubt about this floor light, says Cyril, a splinter, so to speak, that had forced its way under his skin and wandered, and then forced its way out at one point or another and stung, and maybe would sting forever . . .

"That's not what I intended," says Nadine.

"Of course not," says Cyril. "If you intended anything at all, it was to punish the engineer for destroying the lover . . . "

"And so much ado about this?" asks Anatol.

Remembering Menaggio brings us to a theme that has never been sufficiently explored in this house, and in all likelihood it never will be: the difficulties experienced by one individual in relating to another, once it has become clear that individual is merely a collective term for an entire group of personages. It is a bottomless vessel into which many more tears will fall, as Agatha would say, while Anatol concludes anew that the only way to avoid the difficulties of relationships is to avoid relationships—a claim no one has refuted to this day.

"You never know who you might meet," says Dombrowskaya, blowing smoke rings, the hieroglyphics of our fruitless encounters with Dombrowsky; any one of us might meet anyone else, basically we know what is possible:

Nadine comes back from a shopping trip to the city, and instead of her globetrotter she finds a bookkeeper, shabby sleeves worn to a lustrous sheen, talking about expenditures and extravagant costs. Receipts, he says, are the foundation of any well-run household; at the time Nadine laughs, but later she cries, once she realizes that he meant what he said . . .

On the other hand, the globetrotter Dombrowsky, man of the world, spoiled for decades by beautiful women, unexpectedly meets up with Kay, a petulant young girl in disheveled hair and jeans, who has just been digging in the garden and is now chewing on dirty fingernails. It's no wonder, is it, that he slams the door shut and the well-kempt Nadine appears an hour later in the dining room only to find an indifferent everyman who hardly raises his eyes as she enters.

And Penny, who has been looking for Papa throughout the entire house, encounters instead a helpless boy she can't help, and retreats enraged, while Bozena undertakes to console him, talks to him, caresses him, and finally goes into the kitchen to get him a glass of warm milk . . . Unfortunately, when she returns, the boy is no longer there but has been replaced by the monsieur, a gentleman with raised eyebrows who is pouring himself a whiskey and whose mocking amazement forces Bozena into an embarrassed retreat . . .

"We've all had these experiences, haven't we," says Dombrowskaya, "or maybe not?"

Even Cyril: hasn't he taken many a serious problem to a man who didn't even try to hide his disappointment at the fact that Nadine hadn't shown up? Hasn't Agatha, walking in moonlight and reveling in romantic scenes, come upon a melancholy person whom only Vladimir would have been able to help, while Vladimir had just got an inspiration and was dashing it down on the back of an old letter: two arms stretched out toward each other, apparently intending to shake hands, which is impossible because appended to each wrist was not *one* hand but an entire bundle of hands, each one of them reaching for a specific hand, which is also reaching for another . . .

An amusing image to which the various Dombrowskys each react very differently: the art-lover Dombrowsky thinks it wonderful, however, after a thoughtful pause, the husband Dombrowsky says: I ask myself from what distance you view us . . . while the melancholy man in the moonlight turns over the piece of paper and recognizes a love letter he himself has written, he is deeply hurt. Which is why Nadine, who doesn't know anything about all this and is looking for her darling, instead finds an embittered man, who, when she wants to hug him, turns his head away: save yourself the trouble . . . Yes, we know all about this. We sigh in unison, except for Vladimir.

"People from little houses," says Dombrowskaya, "are the only people you can live with, but people from big houses are the only people you want to live with. And then there are the others with whom you neither can nor want to live, they are the ones who are alone in a big house."

We think about Dombrowsky, what he was like when he first met Nadine, the engineer who had subdued, obliterated, and forgotten all of the other Dombrowskys because they inhibited him in his climb, and now that he was on top, suddenly looked around and missed something: hadn't there been someone else here? The battered, shackled, unconscious Dombrowskys came back to him, the ones he had interred in his cellars and storerooms, and for a long time he avoided going home, he traveled around the world and looked for Nadine, as he later told Nadine, but Dombrowskaya doesn't believe this, she believes that he was looking for nothing more than a confederate, a woman with pluck and fantasy to share his fears.

Even at the door, says Dombrowskaya, it smelled like corpses, at least it seemed that way to Dombrowsky when he entered his house for the first time with Nadine. He looked at her out of the corner of his eye and tried to forestall any possible dismay: it smells a little moldy here, he said, that's what happens when you're away for years and the place never really gets aired out . . . That's about to change . . . Nadine didn't notice a thing; she had discovered the world of women. Good God, what glitter! What had she been missing! She had had no idea. To the same degree that Dombrowsky was looking inward, she was embracing the external: jewels, perfume, lingerie, her own unknown body, the reflection in Dombrowsky's eyes . . . She celebrated resurrection every morning.

Nadine in the taxi: she is hardly seated before she takes out her compact, arranges her hair, runs her little finger along the bottom of her lower lip, turns her head to the side and studies the form of her ear, the line of her lashes—as if this were her only natural occupation, and she had wrongfully been kept from it by the presence of others, but is now reclaiming it with great conviction . . .

"Unbearably insipid," says Cyril, "Nadine without the backdrop provided by Anatol. But with it: rather amusing."

Opinions about Dombrowsky are much more varied, much more than, say, opinions about Jeremy, or Viola, to whom we are bound by an inner allegiance, in whom we sometimes see Vladimir, sometimes Anatol, and therefore believe we will never lose them. Dombrowsky, on the other hand, is a stranger, and this is why we are both fascinated and frightened. He was only there when he was there, and when we left him, we left him behind.

In Vladimir's gallery Engineer Dombrowsky is *The Somnambulist*, a man who changes the earth, develops plans, builds bridges, establishes wellheads . . . makes appointments, obeys calendars, sets decimal points . . . An electronic brain that spits out numbers when it is fed questions, no, spits out numbers when it is fed numbers, the kind we see on large bills . . . A man who realizes from time to time that he's doing all of this in his sleep, in the way a dreamer recognizes his dream as a dream, and who, like all dreamers, must finally wake up.

The sleepwalker Dombrowsky wakes up on a November afternoon on a sofa in a room where a conference has just taken place, a room still full of ideas, each of which represents a steely reality he suddenly no longer acknowledges: he knows it is all a dream. What is real is his pitiful, lonely existence, the house in which the entire Dombrowsky clan went down to inglorious ruin solely in order to bring his digital brain to power . . . He sees it clearly; he has never been so awake.

He also sees the secretary come in and circle the sofa, and then, after a glance at his finally awakened face, put her finger to her lips entreating silence from a visitor at the door: not now, he's sleeping, we must let him rest, he needs it badly.

A little later, still awake as never before, he walks through a drizzling rain and, for the first time, he sees live faces instead of faulty architecture, the faces no less faulty but capable of transformation. In front of a café window, under dripping trees, he stops for a face that appears to transform itself under his gaze, a process that fascinates him. Dombrowsky goes inside; a raindrop falls from a leafless branch.

"This was the beginning of the end," says Anatol.

"Only yours," says Nadine. "Thank God."

"From then on everything went shallow."

"From then on everything lit up. Right?" Nadine looks around for support, but we act as if this argument has nothing to do with us, no one takes sides. "You're all very forget-

ful," says Nadine. "Otherwise you'd remember how insuffer-
able Anatol was, especially there in the café, in his last half-
hour, before Dombrowsky arrived . . . "

Indeed.

Anatol, in his last phase, in the afternoon at his favorite
café. As he did every day, he was carrying a newspaper rolled
up in his hand, held somewhat away from his body like a hot
glowing cylinder; he had little hope of reading it: to this day
his every attempt had failed. He sits down near a large window through which he can watch passersby, expecting nothing more of them than that they act out a harmless scene
from life, the everyday. He sees the bustle, the bare branches
of a tree whose name he doesn't know because he has never
seen it with leaves; in summer, he had not yet become a café
regular but found himself driven to work at this hour.

He puts the newspaper down on the table, his hand next
to it in order to share in the cool assurance of the marble. But
the very first glance is a knockout: *Earthquake, 40 Dead.* No,
it's too early to read the newspaper, he still has not learned to
control his imagination, it transports him to an oriental village, chalky white walls, loam, the sun hot, a calm sky, now
the rumbling, a distant thunder, an approaching thunder,
optical aspects shift, lines plunge, surfaces burst, beams splinter . . . He is walking in the street, he is standing in a doorway, sitting in a courtyard, lying on a bed, on a mat, on a dirt
floor . . . wherever he goes, stands, lies—it hits him, wood,
loam, rock, iron, anything of weight hits him in every possible way, muffled, cutting, howling . . . Forty times.

The coffee is here, Anatol reaches for the water glass, with
his handkerchief he wipes the palms of his hands, he fixes his
gaze on the three-column visit by a head of state, an event he
visualizes without consequence, bringing neither harm nor
profit. He feels better, still he must not turn the page: a simple glance at page three means a look into a world Anatol
would never have dared inhabit, had he ever been offered

the opportunity. He can't even read the sports section today, he knows what he'll find: "close to victory" and "out in the fifth round." Beast against beast, the referee a beast employed by beasts, beasts in the auditorium, in the grandstands: exulting.

Stranglers amuck, family tragedies. Anatol in a housing project with a knife in his hand, he waits until his old father comes into the room, runs the knife into the old man's ribs, wipes his hands, goes into the adjoining kitchen and sits down at the table, saying to his old mother: Done for, and the old lady runs toward him with the soup pot in her hand, staring at his lips, because she's almost deaf; yes, but, she says, you always liked this soup . . .

And Anatol next to the little boy on a village street: Get me a Coke, he says. Here's the money, bring it back here and you'll get a little more . . . And then sitting in his room, a strange blank gaze fixed on the doorway where the victim will soon appear, a bottle of Coke in his small pink hand . . . And so on, and on, every day and everywhere, no end in sight . . .

He has put the newspaper down on the chair, now he sees red oozing out of the inside pages, soaking through the first page, flooding over the visit by a head of state, collecting along the edges and dripping onto the floor . . .

This was his last phase, in the afternoon in his favorite café—exhausted from his struggle with the news he couldn't stomach, incapable of pulling himself away, yet brightened by Nadine's approaching presence, which inspired thoughts such as these: It isn't good to be alone. Being alone will make you thin-skinned—batiste, chiffon, and gauze. Anatol was amazed, he hadn't expected to find himself so well informed on the subject of textiles. No one's skin can stay this thin if it keeps rubbing up against someone else's. The constant process of hardening and softening: reproaches and demands, then touching hands and exchanging confidences—this process makes skin supple, but it also makes skin thick: wool, jersey, gabardine . . . There can be no doubt, it was Anatol's chiffon phase that made possible everything to come.

He sipped his coffee, lit a cigarette, crossed his legs and leaned his head to the side and a little back: this way he could observe a drop, which, outside in front of the windowpane, ran along a twig and then stopped suspended; he wondered for how long.

"How could we forget," says Cyril. "It is among our most enduring memories." Nadine doesn't want to believe this. As always when she doesn't know what else to say, she falls back on time as an argument: how can it be that a fleeting apparition like Anatol, a nightmare, she says, a feverish specter, has the same rights as she herself, she who has represented this house for so long . . .

There is nothing to be done for so much naïveté; even Cyril refrains from offering clarification where there is so little promise of success, and only Dombrowskaya is willing to make another attempt. In a subdued voice she provides an account that should free Nadine from her misconceptions, if only Nadine will assent: an entire school age passed by in ten minutes, a lengthy marriage in half an hour, as opposed to the years that flowed away one afternoon around three at a marble table over a cup of coffee . . . And now she's gotten around again to her most cherished concept: "Encounters," she says to Nadine, "are the only things that count. After that, there is only unfolding, evolving. Everything runs its course, you see, or simply leads to another encounter that already contains everything that is to follow. If you leave things at the moment of encountering, you will already have experienced three-quarters of what is to be experienced, indeed the best."

"You can't prove that," says Nadine.

"Think about it," says Dombrowskaya.

Nadine's image made its very first appearance in the retina of a stranger; she was utterly new. He had caught sight of her through a windowpane, on a chair of the comfortable sort, over a cup of coffee and a glass of water, in a red suit with her legs crossed, a cigarette in her hand, her head leaning to the side and a little back, so that she could observe a drop of rain which was about to fall off a branch in front of the windowpane, and so that in order to meet a stranger's glance she had to lower her eyes.

She still knew nothing of herself; it was a moment of divine emptiness. A moment later and she would begin to be aware of herself, she would have surroundings, an origin, a past, in a flash everything created itself out of nothingness and held her firmly in a network of relationships she could not even sense: who was she? Merely someone who was being observed, someone who could float if he weren't seeing her in this chair, someone who for a fraction of a second needed no ground under her feet, so weightless she was, so free.

This is the way it should stay. Would he look away? But he didn't look away; Nadine had begun to become Nadine, objects arranged themselves, her head got a face with origins, she started to resist but she was already ensnared, to her the present seemed to be a perfectly round island of marble, carrying nothing more than a cup of coffee and a glass of water; the only way open to her was the straightaway into the future, but even here details were beginning to emerge, Nadine resigned herself. She turned her gaze back to the drop; she waited for it to fall.

"A moment like this . . . ," says Dombrowskaya, and Nadine must recognize that there's nothing here that can be measured by the hands of a clock. Even Anatol is proof of this: he didn't experience the fall, as far as he's concerned the drop is hanging there suspended forever. But the drop fell, the sign of a provisional finality; Anatol became Nadine and the stranger in front of the window became Dombrowsky, a man who had seen much and then decided, and, what made this so significant, had decided on Nadine.

For years the marble table; coffee, followed by another and finally a Remy Martin . . . Walls that opened exposing vistas, the straightaway into the future, widening to envelop the entire panorama . . .

"Who would have thought," said Dombrowsky.

"No one," Nadine lied. Only slowly, hesitating, they left the café; it was cool outside and it got even colder. Nadine slid her fingers into a muff, they sat in the car and the snow flew at them whirling into tight cones, Nadine stepped on a puddle and it cracked, a web of cracks spread out from her heel, she gave a start, but Dombrowsky smiled and showed her that it was only a shallow puddle and represented no danger at all, the sun melted the snow, drops ran along branches in a hurry to let themselves fall, and while the privet turned green they held hands, Nadine hummed and Dombrowsky whistled a little, then in the gardens and parks leaves crawled out, they walked faster because they suddenly had so much to do . . . July had already roasted the street they were on, Nadine stopped at shop windows until he pulled her along, stopped himself, until she pulled him along, in this way they pulled each other through the empty midsummer city, store windows blinded by the glaring facades of their counterparts turned their gaze into the cool inner reaches of the stores; this did not stop them from going in, selecting, carrying away. You'll remember me, said the clerk. This mattress is so sturdy, you'll still be sleeping on it thirty years from now . . . —and there's already a tear in this dream, it's split at the seams and is surrendering its stuffing of horsehair and foam rubber; Nadine is standing perplexed by the number: thirty? What is thirty years? But Dombrowsky sweeps this danger aside as well, with a nod he initiates the attendant formalities, in an instant the dream is sewn up, they have to hurry now to get to the city office before closing, to say their *I do's*, sign the documents, the engines of an airplane to the south have already whined into life, a breath of the sea on salty cliffs, and back again, the doors to Dombrowsky's house are wide open, it is a much too empty house considering that it is so large, a house that had been uninhabited for so long, Nadine detects a fleeting odor of mold . . .

Faster: the passing of the friendly days, meals and conversations, companionship and quiet, minor differences of opinion ironed out with expressions of tenderness, a profusion of happenings where nothing happens, encounters that are not encounters, even an acquaintance with those Dombrowskys newly brought to life remains nothing more than an acquaintance, up to that day in Menaggio, Nadine in the arms of a new Dombrowsky who is no longer an engineer but only a lover, and who holds everything the other had promised: Nadine among roses, champagne, October, in possession of an endless hour.

And so on, says Dombrowskaya, and so on: Nadine's helpless and somewhat laughable attempt to hold onto that hour, even long after it had passed and time had begun to slip and slide again; life as it was before, only more hurried and with a slightly bitter aftertaste . . . Now, breathlessly on to an encounter that sets off an entire chain of encounters, and in the end will change everything: Jeremy and Bozena on a bench in the park, pitying men's shoes, says Dombrowskaya, an eternal minute. What can no longer be stopped is: the way to Jeremy's hotel, third floor on the right in the garden house, the evening sun on the magnolias only pretending to be magnolias. Then for a long time nothing but Sandra. Well yes, we know, that's a whole life in itself, there isn't enough room for it on the face of a watch. Suddenly it races away as if being hunted through a summer, an autumn, and then lies exhausted one evening: Nadine's bedroom, Dombrowsky's house, a portentous encounter: Nadine, Sandra, Bozena together for the first time, nothing good can come of this, Agatha steps forth offering herself as a temporary solution, but she's not up to handling this crisis, at the last moment Dombrowskaya appears . . .

At this point everything is unwinding so fast that it is hardly possible to keep the details straight: Nadine struggling against Sandra and Bozena, with no one but Penny on her side, and Agatha as the only resting point, who nevertheless, like an anesthetic wearing off, slowly became penetrable; she already felt the draft.

Nadine arriving home at the doorway to Dombrowksy's room: she is happy to see him, she offers him her hands and for a moment she believes everything is all right, will be fine, because Dombrowsky, sitting there at his desk and smiling at her, is everything she ever hoped for in a man, ever dreamed of—she, Nadine, would be satisfied with this one man her entire life—but then she sees her outstretched hands and the small package dangling from one gloved finger: Sandra's perfume, ambergris and myrrh, a fragrance that would only make Dombrowsky shudder, because he loves fresh air and grasses . . . A fragrance for Jeremy.

Nadine lets her hands fall, the room is suddenly full of shards, every step she takes is through splinters, shattered even in her voice as she greets him with words that were true until this moment, but now no longer are . . .

The restless nights upstairs in Nadine's room where Sandra steals across the carpet on tiptoes, Bozena whispers endearments and Nadine runs her ten polished fingernails through her hair, sighing, tossing from side to side and waking up as if dead.

Another encounter: Dombrowskaya at the door to the breakfast room. She has just appeared for the first time in her life, it having just begun, and she carries with her the memories of her predecessors (Nadine, Bozena, Sandra, Agatha, and the others as well) without having to identify herself with them: she is entirely new and autonomous, not overwhelmed by any feeling, not corrupted by any habitual routine.

She liked what she saw without being enthused: the pleasing proportions of the room, brightness filtered through curtains, the furniture in an engineer's house. The table was set near the door to the terrace, the china betrayed Agatha's intervention, while the cuisine recalled Nadine's discreet worldliness: two kinds of ham, cheese, toast and soft-boiled eggs, veal liver sausage and orange jam, coffee and tea. And standing among all this, a newspaper.

"Good morning," said Dombrowskaya. The newspaper sank, the man who had been sitting behind it stood up and said, "Good morning."

So this was Dombrowsky. She recognized his features, indistinct, because he was standing with his back to the light, and they seemed to her neither familiar nor unattractive. A good-looking man, well-educated, an intelligent man. For a moment Dombrowskaya speculated that a friendship with this man would not be without its charms, nevertheless the thought of the conflicts she herself had just now resolved held her back.

"Won't you sit down?" asked Dombrowsky.

"I don't think so," said Dombrowskaya. She could see, even in this light, that he now was wearing a mask. He carefully folded the newspaper as if his involvement with the news of the day were over once and for all. Dombrowskaya wondered who he was missing: he had only known Nadine; he didn't know much about Bozena, and he didn't want to know anything about Sandra. Now at the breakfast table, it seemed for a fraction of a moment that he was calling for Bozena. And she came immediately, as she always did when she was called, but it was too late: Dombrowskaya swept her away. To allow Bozena in, that would mean beginning all over again and ending up the same way once more.

"This is enough," said Dombrowskaya. No one but Dombrowskaya would have dared utter these words. Dombrowsky looked up and a crack appeared in his mask, which Dombrowskaya believed she had heard: an old chest in the night, a pitcher full of ice.

Rage in his eyes as he begins to speak, disappointment and the desire to destroy. He speaks in ribbons of tape that spout from his mouth, they flutter in the wind blowing in through the window. The curtain of what is spoken hangs between them, he tries to see her through the gaps, he fights off the ribbons with his hands, turns his head, stretches . . . He can't see her anymore and he's terrified; in sudden panic he tries to cut through the masses of tape, with abrupt swimming motions he steers through the room, it is useless, he entangles himself in words and fragments of sentences, they wind around him like the tentacles of an octopus, encircle his arms and his legs, ensnare his neck . . . He's immobilized, he wants to sink to the ground, but he can't even do that, the wall at his back resilient, fabric nudging him gently, he staggers, is caught up, sprung back—he doesn't speak anymore, he just sighs and groans, new ribbons of tape full of sighs and groans, and he's finally quiet.

A gust of wind tears a hole in the room. Dombrowskaya sees how he's trying to swallow ribbons, how he's choking . . . He can't do it, he is too short of breath, each gulp of air is only enough for a few letters, it will take him years to swallow the contents of this room, and he won't last that long. Dombrowskaya knows he won't be able to keep quiet for that long, instead he'll start talking again until he chokes . . .

She has retreated back to the wall and is sliding along the wallpaper until she feels the doorknob against her elbow. She opens the door, the wind pulls it out of her hands and smashes it against the wall, a chaos of tape flutters into motion in the direction of the window, the mass is blown away. She can see him again standing in the room exhausted but released, he looks for his words but the room is empty. She steps into the draft of the open door, turns around once more: "Now you go," he says. This tiny piece of tape fluttering on his lips for a brief moment, still questioning, then cut off by his teeth, disappearing in a draft through the window to the outside, is the last she sees of him.

This is the kind of parting that might make us dream, if

Penny had not rushed in full of wrath and misery. She whirls over the carpet like a top, screaming accusations at us:

"It's all your fault! You murdered him! He was my daddy and you drove him away! Now I'll never have a daddy again!" She drops to the floor and crawls howling to the door. There she suddenly becomes silent, stands up, looks around, and declares:

"When I see you my eyes freeze!" With these words she leaves us, but not for long we fear.

Penny. The disposition of this creature is something fearful; terror and destruction appear to be her only goals. We
haven't seen her for a long time and unanimously, as we
rarely are, had hoped that we had gotten rid of her for good,
but now we hear her whimpering on the stairway, and immediately thereafter she reappears in the doorway: with heavy
bandages around her head and hands, a heartrending sight
we no longer fall for. We know her trickery, it's all theater.

Penny walks through the room as if she didn't see us,
humming a little ditty that she prepared specifically for this
appearance:

> My head through the wall
> Huge burns though I'm small
> Your world is a pit full of dangers.
> Everyone's lying
> To me about dying
> Forgetting they, too, are but strangers.

Vladimir applauds because he's enjoying the presenta-
tion, but Bozena allows herself to be taken in this time too,
she hugs the child and consoles her:

"Oh you poor, poor baby! Just wait: by the time you're
grown up everything will be all right!" And this is the opening Penny had been waiting for; she tears herself away and
throws herself to the floor, thus showing her bandages to be
nothing more than props, and imitates Bozena:

" . . . everything old will be good and everything new will be
bad . . . "

"Enough of this show!" roars Cyril, who is the first to lose patience. Penny doesn't know what a show is but assumes from his tone that she's been sworn at; she crawls under the table and pouts.

"She's just a child after all," says Bozena. Still, she is the one who suffers most from Penny's presence. Bozena has only to mention that she has seen a baby in the park, "such a little cutie, little saucer eyes and stubby nose," and Penny is there on the spot, mumbling her litany:

"I was brought into this world, they didn't ask me, they shouldn't have done that to me, they shouldn't be able to do it to anyone, they should stop . . . "

But Bozena will again be the victim of her own compassion.

"In the end she isn't responsible . . . Fundamentally speaking, it's the environment that's at fault . . . "

"Where is the end, where is the fundament?" Penny howls from under the table. "I want to go to the fundament and to the end!" We have trouble quieting her down; training is no longer at issue here: she has had time to learn, but she doesn't want to, so she'll have to learn on her own.

Vladimir has a sketch of Penny in her highchair, a tuft of hair in the middle of her head, tied up with a red ribbon, and a teddy bear in her arms. Mama is stirring a pot of milk on the stove while listening with fascination to the singsong of her baby daughter. In a thin voice, Penny is singing:

> I sense in me catastrophes agrowing,
> My baby days were long but soon will close;
> My blood is black like licorice juices flowing
> I'll stay around for there's no way of going
> I'll be your thorn, let the others try the rose . . .

"What a musical child!" says Mama; she shakes her index finger in fun: "Listen!" The tones of "Babysitter Boogie" ring out from the radio on the kitchen buffet, but come to a sudden halt in the middle of a protracted quack.

Penny sits up in her little chair as if she wanted to look into the pot on the stove, and asks:

"Mama, is dying sad?"

"Very sad, my child."

"Mama, why do we have to die?"

"The reason hasn't been discovered yet, my child; it's just the way things are."

The radio quacks on for a few more beats; the woman bends over the pot to see if the milk has come to a boil. Then Penny again: "Mama?"

"Yes, baby."

"Do we all have to die?"

"Yes, indeed we do my child, that is our misfortune."

Penny throws the bear to the floor, grabs onto the chrome trim of the stove, and stares into her mother's face with an unbelieving and threatening expression only she is capable of affecting:

"Mama—not me?"

"Yes, yes, my child, even you."

Penny lets go of the stove, leans back as far as she can in her chair, observes the woman from behind eyeslits full of perfidy:

"Oh no! And you knew that?"

"Knew?" The mother is amazed. "Knew when?"

"Before you had me," says Penny.

The spoon drops from the woman's hand and her mouth opens to stammer:

"I—yes—why—" and it stays open.

All movement in this picture freezes, even the steam rising from the pot stands inert, then "Babysitter Boogie" rattles and rolls anew, while the milk boils over, flooding the stove, the floor, both figures, and keeps flooding until everything becomes one single white surface . . .

"Quite well done," says Cyril. And Penny says:

"It's just too dumb and stupid."

Penny at a tea party: she brought a penholder she had already behexed—one squeeze and the pen shot out poisonous needles, thin as a strand of hair, almost invisible, thus also unfelt, but deadly without fail, one needle per person.

"Let's give them our cute little hand, and say hello to everyone." So many little handshakes, so many sweet hellos. Penny doesn't curtsy; she may bow if she absolutely must:

"She's a real tomboy. You should see her knee!" Penny calls this the death round; she has her penholder ready. The ladies have barely turned their attention back to their coffee cups when Penny aims her weapon: she shoots like a Sioux, arrow at her shoulder, and incantation must take the place of a bow. One arrow per person, Mama is the only exception: she's not really a grown-up by nature, more through circumstance, one must let her live. The ladies are charmed:

"Puff, puff, we're being shot. Isn't she the cutest little actress!" Penny, conscious of the expended munitions, delivers herself of a correction:

"Mm-e not act, me real!"

"Did you hear that? No, that really is cute: she's not acting, she's real! I'll have to tell Theodor."

The poison is slow-acting. The ladies eat rum-soaked pound cake while praising the coffee and the well-behaved child who is sitting with outstretched legs in an armchair looking at a picture book full of little cats and mice.

"Penny," Mama asks, "you aren't ill, are you?" Why should Penny be feeling ill? The ladies should be feeling ill! But ladies are tough, Penny has already noticed: a man would be much easier to slay.

After an hour her failure is obvious. The poison hasn't worked. Penny leaves the drawing room dragging her feet; this defeat will remain her secret. Not until she reaches the nursery does she allow herself to relax: she writhes in helpless rage on a rug decorated with frogs and daisies. Mama is informed in a whisper that Penny is having another tantrum. Valerian. Now at least it is clear why the child had been sitting so strangely quiet with the picture book. The ladies, drinking their coffee, are full of sympathy: the more sensitive the child, the more difficult the upbringing. In the nursery Mama is busy consoling:

"Once you're a thousand weeks old, everything will be all right." A thousand weeks is still difficult for Penny to comprehend. "Or one yard taller," she says, "like this!"

All Penny needs is one more yard. She would give a lot for one yard: then she wouldn't always have to look up or rely on sometimes faulty magic spells. The child has no inkling what she is wishing for; after growing one more yard Penny will no longer be Penny but Kay, completely transformed outwardly and inwardly, at least as far as a desire to murder is concerned, although we sometimes have our doubts . . .

"It is such a shame," says Bozena shaking her head, "that of all the little girls Penny is the only one still with us. What ever happened to the sweet little dancer?"

We remember her clearly. The little dancer was a skinny thing, eight or nine years old, who seemed to be made entirely of India rubber. For a long time she filled the house with the clatter of her tap shoes on the kitchen tiles, in the rhythm of a popular gramophone record: "*Das ist Berlin, Berlin, die ewig schöne Stadt . . .*" Until the door to the office flew open and Cyril shouted:

"This has got to stop! I can't hear myself think!" Then the clatter stopped, the child sat down on the kitchen floor and enthusiastically stuffed cotton into the toes of her pink shoes; she put on an organdy frock, limped on her heels over to the gramophone, and put on the *Japanese Lantern Dance*, or a selection from the *Nutcracker Suite.*

"It's too bad she's gone," now even Kay agrees.

Acrobatics was the little dancer's specialty; dressed in a blue tricot frock and blue gym shoes, she performed her artful works for us, cartwheel, bridge, splits, and on a holiday we will never forget, a simple backward somersault; she never was able to do a forward somersault.

A happy child with rhythm in her bones and with big plans; she trained every day in front of a walnut chest she used as a ballet bar. Strict commands: "Fifth position! Elever half-toe!"

"She had what it takes to become a ballerina," Dombrowskaya now says, "but unfortunately she allowed herself to be repressed." Her gaze floats so undeliberately through the room that no one of us can feel guilty, and then it alights on Penny.

"She wasn't a strong enough presence," she says.

Suddenly the entire house seems to have nothing better to do than to involve itself in Nadine's prospective activity. Creatures whom we believed to have disappeared show up and give their opinions, unsolicited of course, but seldom unanswered. We were spared Kay, for example, for a long time. But now she's here, adolescent, cool and without mercy, already an expert at departures. A voice like a scalpel.

"You have to preserve that man," she says to Nadine, "that's the best way to get rid of him." We shudder at her words, but we have little to bring against the innocence of her teen years. She is as pure as she is plain, and as plain as she is certain; she knows what she's talking about. This is the way she once finished off Lieutenant Viola, who adorns our house to this day with the lifeless beauty of a mounted butterfly: his voice on tape, his face on photos, his shaving lotion in bottles, and every detail of every encounter noted down—in the end her victim is nothing more than a superfluous by-product of his own relics.

Now she's suggesting this technique be applied to the new admirer: Nadine is to collect souvenirs to use as coffin nails. We don't want to have anything to do with this; Kay is turning our house into a den of murderers.

Kay, a girl in pants, possibly a boy, one can't tell from her figure, and she herself hasn't yet decided, she's standing on the brink: nailed forever to this one summer, to a specific day in June, to a room in a barracks, with a view of barbed wire and letters: STIMIL FFO, or the other way around—OFF LIMITS.

Very far off limits and at the mercy of one particular party: Lieutenant Viola, who at first was nothing more than a tag with an Italian name, and then a back in front of a window, flawlessly tailored and perfectly pressed, against a background of barbed wire and capital letters; at his left shoulder STI, at his right FFO.

What were they waiting for? For the interpreter of course, so the lieutenant could interrogate her. "You know you're not authorized to be in this area . . . that you're not authorized to be outside of your house between eight o'clock in the evening and seven o'clock in the morning . . . You know that we are now under a state of martial law . . . " Martial law means that they can shoot on sight anyone found outside of his house at the proscribed times, especially in these fenced-in areas . . . They don't have to ask any questions, they can simply shoot. If they do decide to ask questions, that means they're looking for something, secret operations, espionage, and then, after they've got what they want . . .

The palms of her hands felt moist, and she wiped them off on her pants. She cleared her throat; if he had forgotten her then he would turn around. He didn't turn around; he kept his hands in his pants pockets, and his shoulders between STI and FFO. Barbed wire ran under his chin and on across his throat. At his right elbow, next to a strip of concrete, grass was growing and waved in the wind. The interpreter kept them waiting.

"I'm afraid," said Kay. "I—am afraid of you." The lieutenant didn't move. His deaf back put words into her mouth. "You can't want that," she said, "you can't want me to be afraid of you, and before I know it I'm going to be ashamed of myself for being afraid of you, but not yet, because I know you can have me shot, you have the power, and we're under martial law, after eight everyone has to be inside his house, but which house am I supposed to be in, I'm a stranger here, and I don't have any house to go to, I'm just passing through. But you don't know that or you don't believe me. You locked me up, and when the interpreter gets here, you'll interrogate me, and you won't believe me, and I'll have to stand here being afraid of you, and it's awful, awful.

"Because I promised myself that I would never be afraid of any person, precisely because it's what they pound into you from childhood on, in school and everywhere, this mistrust of everyone: don't go anywhere with a stranger, they're bad, all strangers are bad, but that would mean that each of us is bad, vis-à-vis anyone who's a stranger, and that we become good simply by becoming acquainted with each other, and that's simply nonsense, isn't it, that can't be true.

"That's why I don't ever want to be afraid of anyone again, it's the first and the last time, and it wouldn't have gotten this far if it weren't for the war . . . the tanks . . . and the barbed wire . . . That's no excuse, of course, and you've got every right to despise me for being afraid of you, as if you were a jungle cat, it's an insult, I'm sorry, and I promise you that the next time I won't be afraid of you, or anyone else either . . . "

The lieutenant turned around. His face was in the shadows, but she saw that he had bent his head back and she guessed that he was knitting his brow. She wiped her hands on her hips again, and then said:

"Excuse me, please." The lieutenant let out a short laugh that might even have been a growl, and began to walk back and forth. As he did, STIMIL FFO became legible again, and the room grew brighter. Lieutenant Viola went to the second window and looked out; he came back to the desk and stopped in front of Kay. She saw Sicily, dusty roads with donkey carts, orange trees, agave, and in between, in a hollow, the sea; she saw Chicago, Al Capone in a Cadillac, a gangster chase over rooftops, a leap into nothingness; she saw, but very briefly, a cart with a "Gelato" sign, and a bunch of balloons; she saw, no, heard Gigli-Caruso on a brilliantly lit stage warbling "la donna e mobile":

"Now, we've had enough of your feeling ashamed," said the lieutenant in a melodic voice, nevertheless in perfect German. "And furthermore, you're wrong: I couldn't have you shot even if I wanted to. And even if I wanted to, I wouldn't, because there'd be too much paperwork." There was a knock at the door, and a sergeant brought in a form. "You see what I mean," said the lieutenant. His laugh seemed frivolous to her.

"If you want," he said, "you can have a job here, in the telephone office. If not, then get out of here, and don't let yourself get caught a second time!" He slapped his open hand with a ruler and watched as Kay chewed on her fingernails. "You don't know where you're going," he said, "or am I mistaken?"

Kay's diary from this time, evidence of noble endeavor:

14 June
    1. Got up too late. Combat sloth!
    2. This mirror over the switchboard: so I don't have to

turn around when someone is talking to me. But no one plays along; they all talk to my back instead of my face in the mirror. Why?

3. The lieutenant usually comes by after work and brings me candy or something like that, sits on my only chair, me cross-legged on the bed. Wants to know everything: where I lost track of my family, who's still left, what I plan to do, what kind of life I'm going to lead. I say: nothing in particular, gypsy. He: that's why I seem so familiar to him. Says that he grew up in a caravan trailer, his parents in the carnival, had a booth where people threw balls at tin cans. Making me envious.

4. Tells me about his girlfriend: Jutta. What's that got to do with me?

18 June

1. More discipline! More concentration!

2. What do I care about Jutta, that she's as dumb as straw and just as blond, greedy as a hamster, only twenty-two and already a widow, been around. I just repeat what the others say, don't know her.

3. Stop biting fingernails!

4. The landlady thinks we've got something going. Absurd, but I'll let her think what she wants.

24 June

My own fault! What I get for being curious. Never again, but it's already too late, have seen her already. Because I know where she lives; no peace since then. Miserable.

Not all that pretty, it's just her long hair and the fact that she's blond, dances around and bats her eyelashes at him, puts on a good show.

I was walking down the other side of the street when she came out of the house with her little weekend bag. She must have said something awfully dumb because he laughed out loud and shouted: "Oh, Jutta!" and that's just it, that's why it's too late, because I can't forget it, the way he said her name, because he could never say my name that way because my name can never be said that way, don't know why.

26 June

1. Missing something. Am I missing something? What?

2. The mirror over the switchboard. Maybe I'm ugly? Of course I'm ugly. Saucer eyes, bangs, no face, only a frame for two moist instruments of vision. That's why they always talk to my back. And otherwise: already eighteen and still no figure, almost none; only legs, and arms like an ape.

3. The newspaper here is looking for volunteers, have applied. There you have to be able to do things, and no one cares if you're blond or if you bat your eyelashes at them.

4. They've gone somewhere for the weekend.

3 July

Jumpy. What's up? Suddenly couldn't take it anymore, yelled at him: Why do you come here anyway? You already have a girlfriend! At first he just grinned, then embarrassed, if anything, said he didn't know himself, maybe because we're both gypsies, no roots, no aspirations, like members of a secret society who recognize each other, etc. Said: That's nothing to you, and that's all right, but if we went out next Saturday? Could that be something? (Because Jutta went to see her parents, he's free.) Terribly nervous now.

10 July

1. Already over with. Be still. Still.

2. We went to Java Junction because people know him around here.

3. Got there at eight, sat, then danced until quarter to one. He brought me to the door and kissed me on the cheek; he said: "It was fun." What's that supposed to mean? He enjoyed it? It was a pleasant little diversion? It was fun . . . And what does he say to her? Oh to hell with it: why am I the way

I am? What isn't right with me? I'm sick of myself, an abomination, intolerable.

There was a candle on our table and I saw for the first time how handsome he is. Like a Roman! That's how I always imagined the Romans to be. He was so nice, always wanting to order something for me: How about another ice cream? Shall we dance? He dances so wonderfully, like a pro, but not me; I let myself be pulled along, can't follow, too reluctant. He has even danced onstage with an itinerant troupe, where the actors have to do everything, even singing and dancing, because there is so little money. Maybe he'd do that again, he liked it, he said, and I said I would, too. "You are my girl," he said, and held me tighter; it was rather dark, only the candlelight from the tables, and the band played "Begin the Beguin," and for one frightful moment, I saw that immense and wondrous something that I had been missing, and anyone missing that was missing an entire life, what I wanted most of all was to throw my arms around his neck and beg him not to leave me, eyes unopened, unfulfilled, but it was already over, the end of the dance, we went back to the table, and I looked around, all of the women were Juttas, all of them acting alike, cooing, ogling, hugging, a foreign language, I don't understand one word and I never will, I'm dumb to this great palaver, I am shut out.

16 July

1., 2., 3. I must be crazy. What I do at work when there's nothing to do: I call him up. During the day when he's not at home. I don't want to talk to him, I only want the phone to ring in his room, a room I've never seen. Now I see it, each time more clearly: how it fills up with ringing, at first only the air from floor to ceiling, then, more slowly, the drawers and chests, and finally it is saturated; the carpet drinks it in, it soaks up into the drapes, into the upholstery; wood takes a little longer, it must repeat its shrill assault again, a few more times before the varnish shatters into minute cracks, like overfired china, and becomes permeable . . . His room is drunk with my ringing, it's even swaying a little. That is my goal: that he comes into this drunken room in late afternoon, looks around, and notices that something has changed. And something really has changed. Before it was empty, now it is loaded. Has someone been here? he thinks. And slowly the room transfers its tension to him, my ringing . . .

4., 5., 6. I must be crazy. What I do in my room in the evening: I pray in reverse. I don't say: free me from my sins, but: free the others from their sins and give them to me. Or, if that won't work: free me from the sins I have and, in return, give me the ones I don't have. I offer heaven a deal, and I won't be outbid: three sins for two, I say, make it four. Four sins for two, no, for one single sin. Every sin I have, or ever will have, for just this one.

7. Things can't go on like this.

19 July

Already trapped. Now I know how it's done. Asked him, for the first time, for a present, and it really was a present: a record with his voice on it; you can get them made here. Now I play it downstairs in the living room when the landlady isn't there. It sounds like a telephone conversation: "Hello, is that you, my little gypsy girl?" Most of what's on there is nonsense, sometimes when he can't think of anything he even whistles; but it is his voice. I'll tape it and then I'll have it forever. I also have two photos and a recording of "Begin the Beguin"; the only thing missing is his shaving lotion, and I already know which one he uses, only have to pick it up. Then I can play Java Junction as often as I want. Then he won't have to come anymore.

22 July

Dreamed: I was standing in front of his room, saw the door clearly in spite of the darkness, the grain of the wood was like rings of water that flow away from each other and then back together; I opened it and it creaked. A warmth and a scent I couldn't recognize escaped from the room. I felt for the light switch with my left hand around the right side of the door frame. Then I touched a strange hand already there. I pulled back, and just as the light went on inside, I slammed the door so hard that a piece of plaster fell from the ceiling; it broke over my head but I hardly felt it, it was wafer-thin or like paper.

28 July

1. The newspaper asked me to come in for a test, went well.

2. Dare to have some hope, but already know: it has to happen. The other way is closed off, slammed the door myself. Didn't I?

31 July

1. Gave notice; starting on 1 September at the paper, got it in writing.

2. They got me a room in town, huge by comparison. Everything's going to be different, *I'm* going to be different.

3. The new landlady's name is Frau Stieglitz.

2 August

1. Evening. So that's the way it is. I still don't understand.

2. Night. So that's the way it was.

He sat on the chair, typical: crossing one leg over the other, held the ankle of his right foot in his left hand. He asked me if I'd be interested in going with him to the U.S. in October. I asked him if he'd like to come with me to the newspaper in September. We laughed; he said: Your offer is a joke, mine isn't. Wasn't meant to be a joke, he wanted to say. I asked: Why? What for? Why me and not Jutta? One of the answers, I thought, will make everything possible. I thought about Java Junction. He raised his hands and said: Oh, Jutta! That's something entirely different! Don't I know. It's the language I don't understand. He will never say my name that way. I said: No, never, and he got up. He smiled as he left.

3. I have the picture, the lotion, the voice; I don't need him.

4. They say you get over it.

"Simply revolting," says Cyril, "This self-righteousness. She doesn't need him! That's all she cares about; never thinks about him, only about herself. The good Viola has no idea how lucky he was to have been spared this iceberg . . . But she was always that way," he says, leafing through the first pages of Kay's diary, "cold and self-righteous. Like here, when she was just fifteen! You should hear this:

> 'Sunday. Went to church. Sermon: thou shalt not kill. Totally shocked. What kind of creature is man that he has to be told something like this? Thou shall not kill, steal, lie . . . As if this kind of behavior were somehow normal! Disgusting. Are we supposed to feel proud about being one of the species? Can't.
>
> And love, a panacea: keep people from killing each other on the one hand and secure the survival of the species on the other. Of all species, this one! No, not interested in love.
>
> P.S. I consider the Ten Commandments to be the most humiliating document in the history of mankind. If this isn't a generally accepted view, then it's only because everyone feels he's being addressed. Do I feel this concerns me? No.'"

"Not bad for fifteen," says Dombrowskaya. "You can see that she's already thinking independently."

"And that she's as pure as an angel, ashamed and repulsed by the weaknesses of her kind; not inclined to feel herself included among them. Aloof." And why not? We keep our silence. Kay has folded her arms and is watching him, her eyebrows raised.

"Aloof and forgetful," says Cyril, "because here I have another little page, the counterpart so to speak, written six or seven years before, can't tell for sure, because in addition to leaving out the punctuation she's also left out the date, but there's no question that it's in Penny's hand:

> 'My matchbox is almost full I will be the first one with a full matchbox but wasn't a very good idea flies legs are very tiny have to find the big ones. half wasps would be better fill up the matchbox faster caught eight today in raspberry juice. wished auntie gugula dead because she told mama pennys going to be a real handful she should fall in a coal cellar full of broken glass and spiders that will suck her blood out the way they suck it out of flies . . . '

And so on, this and that, mangled nightcrawlers, tormented babies, squashed frogs . . . "

"Right!" shouts Penny, having listened, enthralled. "Tiny little frogs, always when it rained, by the pond, the whole road was full of them! I got at least three with every step, once I got five, and that's with my little shoes, not like yours . . . " She takes off one sandal and shows us the sole; we ourselves are amazed that five frogs at once could have left their lives behind on such a small surface. "But that's just it," Penny says modestly. "They were so new and teeny tiny."

"What did I tell you!" says Cyril.

He's right, as is so often the case, and it would have been best to leave things at that, especially since only Kay is directly involved, and Kay, for her part, still doesn't feel it's any of her business, so she says:

"I really don't know what you expect—she's your Penny as much as mine!" But Bozena, who simply can't resist when she sees a creature in distress, begins to defend Kay, showing the immensity of her goodwill to bear no relationship to her powers of persuasion; all of her arguments are based on the precept of Kay's grand youth: "She is still so much a child . . . so inexperienced . . . ," stammering up against Cryil's mocking grin and Kay's contempt, until Dombrowskaya interrupts, less to help Kay, about whose nature she harbors no illusions, than to finish the discussion off cleanly; she has a deep aversion to feelings in their raw state.

She presents a picture of Kay's situation: the girl who has just outgrown childhood, and having discovered the ideals of humankind has committed herself to following them, who nevertheless feels frustrated in her progress because she is hauling Penny's skin around like an itchy, formless eggshell she has just burst through and can't discard. Poor Kay: she wants to feel the wind of a new existence in her face, but what she senses is a draft on the sensitive areas behind her ears, which haven't yet had time to dry off—and Penny, over and over again: Penny as an octopus clasping her with countless tentacles, making it hard for her to breathe; Penny as a nightmare on her back, a burr in her hair . . . Kay's life is a series of courageous attempts at escape, the struggle of one who desires the Good-Beautiful-True against the forces of darkness.

"And signs of Penny everywhere," says Dombrowskaya, "in every drawer, in every book: the devil's twisted face with a flicking tongue, portraits of witches and curses, all of which portend no good, circles drawn around monograms shot through with arrows or stuck with needles, and among these, diary pages like the ones just noted . . . In her beginnings Kay was occupied with annihilation, with clearing off and burning: the work of an exterminator."

"An undeserved defense," says Cyril.

"I don't mean to say," says Dombrowskaya, "that she enjoyed success in her undertakings," and Penny pops out from behind her chair making a face at Kay.

"Nevertheless," says Cyril, "simply repugnant, her self-righteousness."

We've come full circle; it seems that we never learn a thing.

Strangely enough, most of us detest our predecessors, who in a way are our origins! Why can't we ever admit it? Dombrowskaya wonders why Cyril has so little sympathy for Kay, Kay wonders why she hates Penny (although this should come as no surprise to anyone), and Anatol admits what he has felt all along: that he can't stand Cyril. Nadine despises Anatol, but no one despises Nadine, Bozena, or Sandra. That's because Dombrowskaya is more thoughtful than the rest of us and is not interested in despising anyone.

She also has an explanation: we dislike our predecessors because they represent stages we have passed through, and we are insulted to find them still here; actually an impudence . . . We don't really understand until we see our successors: they think exactly the same way.

"You make me tired," says Nadine. "What I'd like to do right now is take a little nap." She's gotten clever all of a sudden! She wants to get rid of us. In her sleep she's by herself, dreams are dreamed alone and they're not shared until we wake up, assuming we remember them. Anyone who doesn't want to share a dream will have to forget it.

Nadine is hoping for a beautiful dream, and she's not intending to forget it: she'd rather have it dissected by the others; it will endure, a dream in spirits as it were, chopped up but everlasting.

Unfortunately, we can't allow that.

"You can't sleep now," says Dombrowskaya, "it's already six. In two hours you'll be picked up, and by then you have to be clear about what you are going to do . . . "

"It *is* clear to me, but apparently not to you . . . "

"Nonsense," says Dombrowskaya, "it's one and the same." She toys with her cigarette holder, a sign that she's deep in thought. "And what if we don't even let you out of the house? If we invite him in instead?"

"Splendid!" shouts Cyril, "that's the best idea I've heard today. That way we keep Nadine under control, and there's absolutely zero risk . . . "

"You're so right," says Nadine, "because I won't be there." A silence falls over us, we're aghast; we've never seen her so determined. Maybe we went too far this time? Fortunately Vladimir is ready to begin a performance: "Nadine's Rendezvous in Nadine's Absence." He's going to save us.

This is how Vladimir imagines the visit of the young man: Cyril in the living room across from him has just heard about the latest trends in contemporary literature, employing an exaggeration of the concrete in order to break through the boundaries of the concrete, when the young man interrupts himself in the middle of one of these abstract phrases, holding his breath in and his mouth open, as well as his eyes, which have just fallen on Sandra's portrait, hanging in a round frame over the sofa: the typical example of a picture that has taken hold. Cyril watches him with a smile.

"You find her attractive?"

"Who was she?" the young man asks, without taking his eyes off Sandra.

"She still is," says Cyril, but here he sees he has made a mistake: the young man leaps up, and it wouldn't take much to make him grab Cyril by the lapels and demand to find out where she is, where he can find her . . .

"Please," says Cyril, "how could I do that to you! Be satisfied with the picture. I'm giving you good advice, you'll get more from it—and for a longer time."

"I don't need your advice!" yells the young man, who seems to have been robbed of both his reason and his good manners by the vision of Sandra. "I need this woman's name, her address, any point of reference . . . I pray you"—here his rage turns to distress and for Cyril it is time to go—"it can't make any difference to you, just her name . . . "

"Never!" says Cyril as he turns to the door. After taking two steps he hears the changed voice of the young man behind him:

"Who does this guy think he is, anyway!"

Cyril turns around and replies with a measured bow:

"I beg your pardon, I don't know what you mean."

"Disgusting fantasies," says Nadine. She stands up, takes her handbag, and looks toward the door as if she wanted to leave.

"Not interested in staying, are we?" asks Vladimir. We laugh; the question is an old one. Still Vladimir is the only one of us who doesn't take sides. He observes us like a stranger from a distance, it's all a game to him, no matter what happens to us.

"Things would be different," says Nadine, "if there were no men in this house. They make everything so confusing. And, what's more, they take advantage of us for their own purposes: Cyril's occupation, Anatol's suffering, Vladimir's play . . . " Her animosity toward Cyril and Anatol is breaking through again. "You two," she says, "have stolen years from me, years! The least you can do now is leave me in peace!"

"We're not doing anything to you."

"But you're there! That's bad enough!"

"It's our house as much as it is yours; you can go if you don't like it." She knows that she cannot, or at least that she would always have to return. There is no other refuge.

"I'm staying," she says, as if she were free to decide, "and I will assert myself—against an entire house full of men, if need be . . . " She sits down again, but the atmosphere remains tense.

Dombrowskaya tries to divert attentions. The combining of personages, she says, is itself a game, and an exceptionally amusing one at that. She paints a picture of how things would be if, for example, only Vladimir and Sandra lived in our house. What a team! What potential! Might there ever have been such a combination before?

Cyril finds the thought absurd: a predatory beast with a sense of humor simply doesn't exist, it would play with the hare instead of devouring it. That is: first Vladimir would play with it, then Sandra would devour it; or the other way around: first Sandra devours the hare, and then Vladimir draws a sketch of it from memory . . .

Anatol is repulsed: to lure a hare with tricks and then devour it, or the other way around, to make fun of one's victim . . . "Vicious," he says, "vicious." Vladimir himself remains quiet: he can't think of anything to add, and questions of morality are beyond his competence.

But Cyril has been inspired, he constructs endless combinations, some of which appear to be fatal—Penny and Anatol, for example: "That would be the end of us." With combinations of threes and fours he could spend weeks. Anatol tells him that the combinations are almost endless, so Cyril limits himself to a personal wish: Anatol, Vladimir, and himself—that would be a trio! We keep quiet. Agatha folds her hands at the thought of so much intelligence paired with so much sensitivity and wit. Bozena can hardly keep from laughing.

"There, you see," says Nadine, "a house full of men, that's what they've always wanted." Suddenly Kay jumps in:

"So what?" she asks. "Three men together are nowhere nearly as dangerous as one Sandra!"

Sandra is different. She has never known worries like Nadine's, worries about a wrinkle on her neck or an extra inch around the waist. Sandra is like an undertow; an undertow knows nothing of itself. And that's why we know so little about Sandra. She is the only one of us whose experiences are not always, and never completely, available to us. Whatever is reported about them, we know: there is more. There is something that cannot be captured, either in Cyril's protocol or in Dombrowskaya's perspective. There's something in the wind.

It will remain a mystery to us, why she first appeared with Jeremy, in that garden room, which until so recently had sheltered Bozena's gentle spirit, and the lyrically frivolous shimmer of the false magnolias. Jeremy, seen through Sandra's half-closed eyes, must have looked like an hors d'oeuvre: pale-skinned, fine-boned beneath the ketchup of his hair— and fearful, not of her, not yet, but of others out there; a Jeremy who, when he sits in the car, fogs up the window with his breath, because he can't stand the gaze of the passersby, who invents a thousand lies for the sole purpose of leading the pack astray, who, like a squid, hides his every trace in inky darkness.

Maybe it was just that. He stood behind her in the room and smiled at her, without reply. Sandra cannot smile; she cannot laugh either; everything about her is black-blooded and somber. Jeremy held his smile in spite of this; more to the point, he held himself up by his smile; it was a smile like an outstretched arm holding her away, but only for a short span of time, for as long as it takes an arm to get tired.

No one knows what she saw when she looked at him; maybe she didn't see anything, but merely obeyed orders sent her way, but not very likely: Sandra's orders don't come from any external source, they are part of her organism, inseparable, ingrown, spleen, liver, pituitary gland.

She remained completely still: her head hung back; her face, released from any possible affinities, no longer allowed for comparisons. What was observable was of minor significance: the narrow slits of her eyes, the turned-down corners of her mouth; a rhythmical flaring of nostrils being the only dynamic detail.

As his smile disappeared she walked past him to the bed and undressed, slowly, surely, piece by piece, a being on its way to its true state. She climbed out of her clothes and lay down naked on a stranger's bed, like the first best whore. No, not even this comparison would do: when Sandra lay down naked on Jeremy's bed, her hands folded under her head, and her feet slightly parted, then it was not like a whore, it was like Sandra; nothing else.

He didn't come closer but reached for his tie instead, like a man afraid he will suffocate, or like a man who is undressing because a woman is lying on his bed. He stopped with the tie, because an almost imperceptible beckoning in Sandra's eyes invited him to come closer, and here the expression *almost imperceptible* immediately shows itself to be nothing more than a necessary convention of reporting: at this moment, in which the boundary between perceptible and imperceptible became hopelessly blurred, for an extended time, or simply unimportant. The fact is, things came to a halt with the tie because Sandra, though she didn't know it then, loves the feel of suiting on her bare skin.

The chestnuts already stood in the shadows.

"Love," said Jeremy, "is when we can no longer make arrangements." Sandra said nothing. Responding is not part of her repertoire; all impulses originate with her, from within her bowels, initiating reactions to which she reacts. She only responds to responses.

A new impulse:

"More," she said.

Events didn't come to an end with the tie. She also loves the feel of skin on her skin, though she didn't yet know it. Everything Sandra knows she knows since Jeremy.

The chestnuts lay in darkness.

"Love," Jeremy said, "is when we no longer want to escape."

"Fine bones," said Sandra. Words that cracked, cannibalistic words. She had her fingers on his wrist.

Everything Sandra is she has become since Jeremy.

Words didn't mean much to her. She considered *betrayal* and *fidelity* to be nothing more than intellectual diversions, mind games. Sandra stayed true to Sandra and couldn't possibly behave any other way; according to the standards of currently accepted usage, she was true to Jeremy; according to a finer standard applied by Jeremy, she betrayed him with everyone, and everyone with everyone else, which is to say:

Walking along the street when she, Circe in the midst of her herd, let herself be carried away by lascivious stares; while shopping in a store, feeling the breath of a stranger on the back of her neck, her eyes immersed in the gaze of a clerk; in the evening at a party, where she succeeded in optically peeling off her dress and suddenly appeared bare except for a pair of delicate sandals, a glass of champagne in hand, in polite conversation with an elderly gentleman from Peru, she was the target of every eye in attendance. And so on: sunbathing in a beach chair lounge, when every square inch of her body became an expression of surrender, for which "sensual" was an inadequate description and "sun" a laughable motivation . . . etc., etc.

It was only with Dombrowsky that she never betrayed him. From time to time she brought one of her admirers to

Jeremy, sometimes she brought two, remarkable beings who obeyed her every command and seemed to have no will of their own. She fetched them, so to speak, and laid them at Jeremy's feet, and when he stepped back in disgust, she looked up at him submissively, and said: "Here. All for you. Enjoy your triumph!" And loathsome as she was, Jeremy found her irresistible.

Jeremy changed his behavior; of his own free will he began to tell her about his daily routine, even talking about his plans for the following day; he gave up his protective game of hide-and-seek, never engendering anything but polite interest from her. These details meant nothing to Sandra; once she was in possession of her prey, no lie was possible. Jeremy was a fool who began to understand that he was a fool, and, more importantly, that this insight was of absolutely no use to him. He helped himself with laughter, but his previous state of being was no longer attainable.

"Jeremy and Sandra," says Dombrowskaya, "my God, what an image! A man who has spent his life disguising his life, who invented a panopticon full of Jeremys for the sole purpose of distracting the viewer's attention from his real self, relentlessly occupied with the construction of Potemkin villages in order to mislead his pursuers, a man who guarded every detail of his past like a jewel, who secretly, a miser, wallowed in his treasures—there was a whole sack full of facts that were never allowed to become information . . . Then Sandra appears and he wants to give her everything he has, his most precious possessions, he's no longer afraid, he pours out the jewels in front of her, and says: here, for you! And Sandra looks at them and sees that they are nothing but gravel. Jeremy has been hoarding a pile of stones. Bared of his lies, Jeremy is neither a victim nor a sensation, nothing but a man who had been frightened for no reason at all, a plucked bird of paradise . . . "

No one knows how it ended, or why. From the time

Jeremy fell ill everything turns to shadows. All we have is a minor scene in the lobby of Jeremy's hotel, which appears to be an echo of one of his first stories: Sandra and the desk clerk, between the potted palm and the cagelike elevator.

It's about key number fifteen. The key is there and yet not there, simply because it no longer has any function: it will of course open the door, but the room is empty.

"You're welcome to see for yourself," says the desk clerk, and without looking up reaches for key number fifteen.

"No, thank you," says Sandra. She already knows. The clerk shrugs his shoulders and hangs the key up again.

"No messages?" she asks.

"I'm sorry."

"No forwarding address?"

"I'm sorry."

Sandra gazes down at her feet; if she stays here any longer her feet will become as anonymous as the hallway. She takes them away. The elevator, open-mouthed, grins idiotically. The desk clerk bows. The palm expresses its sympathy as Sandra leaves.

She was still with us when we moved into this house, an extraordinary being, old-fashioned in her obsession, she possessed more impetuousness than the rest of us combined. Early in the morning she would leave the house, where she did not feel comfortable, and would run hungrily through the streets, her eyes seeming to be locked on a trail, no consideration for the rest of us, who had to suffer because of her: she does after all share our name. But even with all her depravity there was a certain greatness about her; it wasn't security she was seeking, it was danger, she had made the city her jungle and ran light-footed along its paths, a beast on the prowl, said Cyril, but Dombrowskaya disagreed: anyone hunting for prey will not have long to hunt; prey, she said, shrugging her shoulders, is everywhere, but Sandra was seeking something different: an abyss. "She has an irresistible urge to plunge over the edge," said Dombrowskaya, and we turned pale.

An abyss is a rare thing; she soon became weary of the plains and gentle slopes. She disappeared.

At first, her absence went unnoticed, but it wasn't long before everyone had heard. We met in the living room as if by accident, every one of us occupied with thoughts of her loss, although no one dared use the word *loss*, as long as some of us viewed Sandra's disappearance as a liberation. Even Vladimir remained exceptionally somber, for a while he just stood around in the room, an alien body among pieces of furniture who succeeded again and again in turning pieces of furniture into alien bodies, as he did this time, too: he simply waited until they were unmasked, exposing their purpose as pure pretense, showing them to be nothing more than the laughable junk they were—any stone, any crate, any tree stump could have taken their place—then he went to the window, rested his chin on his hand, and looked out.

Agatha, who certainly is not malicious, just abundantly dumb, suddenly started to blather on: what a blessing to finally be rid of the young lady, one never knew what to expect from her, one single person like her could completely destroy the reputation, even the existence, of a good house, and so on. She used expressions such as *refuge* and *security* and confessed that as long as this *vagabond* was in the house, she would hardly dare step out onto the street because she might be taken for *one of that sort* . . .

"That was a needless worry, dear child," said Dombrowskaya. Most of us laughed; Cyril waved his hand, saying:

"Apart from Agatha's nonsense—I'm also happy that she's gone. She upset us, she disrupted my work." Dombrowskaya said endearingly:

"You're right, but if I'm not mistaken we all disrupt your work." Before the conversation could take its usual turn toward altercation, Vladimir turned around and said:

"We miss her!" We had no time to feign surprise. He was

so very right; we missed her. And how we missed her! Never, so it seemed to us, had we missed anyone the way we missed Sandra now. Even Cyril knew it, even Agatha.

"But she'll come back," said Vladimir, "we can't lose her." We stared at him; we could have kissed his hands, we were that grateful.

We joke about Jeremy.

"Now he's a skeleton in Sandra's closet, we hear him rattling in the night."

"I'll say, it's his teeth chattering in fear."

"He could do that even before his skeleton phase!"

"No wonder, knowing Sandra . . . "

"But she never really did anything to hurt him, he was simply afraid of the tracks he found . . . "

"Poor Sandra. He made her despise virtue."

"Poor Jeremy."

"Hear ye, hear ye, Bozena still cares!"

"He'll wilt away if there's no one to take care of him."

"If anyone tries, he'll wilt even faster."

"You said he was already in the closet! And he's rattling! Well, hand him over!"

"Oh no, Penny, he's no toy, that's just a figure of speech, go away and pen a little poem."

"Jeremy, forever Jeremy! This is where our new life begins, and all you can talk about is Jeremy."

"Nadine is right; this will have to stop. And it's not Jeremy's skeleton rattling around in the closet, it's ours."

"Cyril is the brightest one, again: of course, it's our own skeleton! The only person in this house we can count on . . . "

"Ooh, ooh," groans Agatha.

When Cyril gets back from the newspaper, he behaves in a most interesting way: He unlocks the door, and then, looking neither to the left nor to the right, he goes straight to his desk. There he rests his chin in both hands and stares at the wall, turning his arrogant back to the rest of us.

At this point we say nothing and communicate through signs; we find it simply absurd the way Cyril inflates his importance when returning from the outside: he forgets that he is only a reporter, who, noting the happenings in our house, assembles them in a more or less believable fashion and sells them in installments. That's how we make our living, very modest, it's true, but a living nonetheless.

But this work spoils him, too. The editors laugh incredulously when he confesses that his stories are nothing but factual reports. "Why should you belittle the achievements of your fantasy?" asks Stranitzky's assistant. "Your worthy modesty aside, if you want us to believe that these stories are nothing but reports about your experiences, then that's going too far." Cyril is blushing, the editor takes this to be another sign of modesty, but in reality it's just the unearned praise that is embarrassing Cyril: "If you don't want to accept it as a report," he says, in a feeble attempt at dissent, "then please view it as a particular interpretation of the facts . . . it's definitely not fantasy." The editor laughs out loud at this, and calls in the second assistant, who joins in heartily. Cyril protests no more. "Tell me," the second assistant says sanctimoniously, "when do these things occur to you?" "Always when I'm alone," Cyril lies, and thereby avoids blushing again, "alone at home, alone in the city, alone in the world . . . " To his amazement he sees that this preposterous claim finds acceptance with both men and results in neither laughter nor consternation: "There you have it," shouts the second one triumphantly, "now you're admitting it yourself you're alone: proof that the others exist only in your fantasy!" Apparently he feels it is possible for a person to find himself alone in the city and alone in the world, just as he feels it is possible for someone to be sitting alone in his room.

Cyril is only human: if people keep telling him these things long enough, he begins to believe them himself; he feels himself a poet and accepts acclaim especially for those parts that are obviously Vladimir's, or even Anatol's. Proud as a peacock, he goes home and succeeds for a time in regarding us merely as freaks of his fantasy, no, as the products of his creative powers, until we show him better . . .

We show him better. But first we take pleasure in playing along for a while. Anatol expels a melodic sigh.

"Just happy," he says, "that I'm no real person; a life like mine is barely tolerable as invention—as real life it would be impossible! Hopefully it will stay this way . . . Don't really know, but sometimes, in a funny way, it seems so real to me: add a bit of milieu, a couple of characteristics, a few prejudices, and I seem to me to be a person!"

"That's as it should be," says Cyril to himself, as he thinks, and jots down *milieu* on a slip of paper.

"I," Vladimir now says, "would like to lodge a complaint: I am not developed well enough, not rounded out enough, no dimensionality. This might suffice for a human, there are dozens of half-baked specimens running around on the streets, but for a character in a novel it's inadequate, it requires depth and definition . . . I'm afraid," he says, tearing at our heartstrings as he sobs into his handkerchief, "I have been created by an incompetent!" And Cyril, who is still sitting at his desk, goes so far as to consider this ecumenical merriment his own.

Suddenly, Bozena is moved.

"There's something childlike in this," she says, "naive conventional wisdom. We might almost be envious."

"Yes, yes," shouts Nadine, "that's it: I envy him! I would like to be able to be an individual too, and not just for one moment at a time. I certainly need it more than he does, or at least I'd get more out of it!"

"We can't even be angry with him," says Dombrowskaya. "After all, it's the simplest solution and has been in use for so long; the common denominator that facilitates communication with the outside world."

This is Anatol's cue; he has forgotten Cyril and playing along, he is possessed of a theory, an analogy, which is driving him to distraction because he cannot find a way to make it comprehensible to us: the super sign! The only concept that can adequately describe our situation, our problem, our possibilities. One word like gold, he says, and, if you only had a minimum of mathematical understanding! One single ounce! But what does he expect in a house full of women, he's in the wrong place, as he can see, wasted, he almost wants to say, although this sounds arrogant, but it would be no surprise if he became embittered, at least maybe Vladimir will understand, even though his head is full of nothing but foolery, or maybe Cyril, who's sitting at his desk thinking himself a poet . . .

Anatol, filled with a passion he otherwise conceals, announces that we are the best possible example of information theory, something we have never heard of. Our unit can be measured in *bits*, he claims unchallenged, and given the current count of entities in this house, the information value of each individual will have to be expressed in terms of binary ten, that is to say, three and one-third bits, or something of the sort . . .

Where it is always a given, he adds, that each of the ten individuals appears an equal number of times, a requirement that fortunately remains within the realm of the theoretical, he says, with a sideways glance at Sandra and Agatha, purely theoretical . . . At this point no one dares interrupt Anatol, now on a roll, pacing back and forth across the room, taking a hand off his hip from time to time in order to point out a formula gleaming brightly in his eyes but not in ours.

This is why it is obvious, he claims, that Cyril, at his desk and thus in this house, can only be represented by the binary value one, while the article lying on the desk, encompassing us all, so to speak, can only be understood as a super sign with a binary value of ten, or perhaps nine, should one of us, for example, Sandra, not appear, though this is highly unlikely.

"It really is very simple," says Anatol. "I'm sure you must have understood." And no one dares enlighten him.

A super sign is what any one of us becomes when he leaves the house as an individual, representing a complete I, which whether we like it or not includes us all . . .

"Binary ten," says Vladimir, "we've had that before."

"Y-y-yes, now," exclaims Anatol, "because we are ten at this very moment! But how were things before? Consider this for just one moment!"

We consider. Cyril and Vladimir see associations, but no one dares approach the binaries.

Kay, for example, says Anatol, what information value do you think she had for Lieutenant Viola? Kay frowns and shrugs her shoulders, indicating how little meaning such computations hold for her. Binary two! shouts Anatol, because at that point in our development, besides herself, Penny was the only additional personage Kay contained, somewhat too few, but hardly her fault.

By the time we get to Jeremy things have changed: when he met Nadine he was encountering what had already become a binary value of five, with the addition of Bozena it's binary six, and with Sandra, binary seven. Big numbers, aren't they . . . And finally there's Dombrowsky!

And this is where mathematics becomes tragedy. He was so happy with a Nadine of binary five, while the successive values of binary seven and—including Agatha—binary eight became a pure hell for him, and once we get to binary nine, which Dombrowskaya brought about with her appearance in the breakfast room, his only possibility was to be left behind . . .

"Stop it," screams Nadine, "this is too awful!"

Cyril, who is still sitting at his desk, suddenly says:

"I'll be damned! I believe I know more than I know!" and never once considers the erupting merriment to be his own. On the contrary, he leaps up and slaps Anatol on the back. "If you had only told me this before, those editors wouldn't have gotten the best of me, not the first one, not the second one . . . "

"And I've hardly gotten started." Anatol pauses, and we can

see he's getting sad again, the impossibility of explaining these theories to us depresses him. "Entropy, for example . . . " It is a lovely word, but no one encourages him to continue; only Dombrowskaya inquires if she is correct in her assumption that with increasing binary values the number of potential conflicts also increases, a question Anatol cannot answer because it is not a problem of mathematics but of human behavior. Vladimir responds in his stead. "And how," he says, "and how." We are surprised; we've always thought he was very funny, but not especially sensitive: what does he know about conflicts?

When Vladimir gets an inspiration, he'll use any available medium, a visual illusion, pantomime, painting and poetry; he has even been known to sing. His performances are never set for any particular time of day, whoever happens to be in his presence can watch, the rest of us are out of luck, there are no encores. Vladimir performs for his own enjoyment (*breadless art* says Cyril, *luxury,* says Dombrowskaya) and doesn't care about applause. We are not his audience, we are his raw material.

Today, he happens to be a man in black on a black stage. Sitting on one lone piece of furniture, a chair, letting his hands hang loosely between his knees, staring at the floor. Nothing is happening.

Suddenly he makes a great leap into the air and lands softly on the floor, which must be made of steel; grins triumphantly. Then he lowers himself to the floor on one knee and hammers the steel with his fists; the steel does not give. The man stands up pleased with himself, sits down on the chair, holding his body straight, his feet spread apart, hands on his hips, elbows rotated forward.

A red bud appears in the middle of the steel floor. The man's body trembles, he jumps up, retreats behind his chair, and with wide-open eyes he watches the bud grow and open into a blossom without leaves, without a stem. Beads of sweat appear on his forehead.

The bud releases one spiraling carmine-red petal after another. And slowly raising the chair high over his head, the man is about to send it crashing down onto the blossom; then he simply puts it back where it was. He shrugs his shoulders and rubs his eye sockets with his fists. He lets his fists fall away and sees: the blossom is still there. It is no longer growing, it is just standing there, harmless perhaps, poisonous perhaps, carmine red for sure. The man gathers his strength, takes a deep breath, leaps onto the blossom, steps on it, and squashes it with his heel, full of rage, thoroughly, until the last petal is crushed.

The floor is clean and smooth again, not a single scratch remains. The man drops his arms and exhales. He glides back to his chair on tiptoes, touches it, quickly sits down, pulls up his knees and embraces them with his arms while anxiously studying the floor, the walls, the ceiling . . . He trembles.

"There you have it!" shouts Nadine. "He agrees with me!"

"What should we think of this?" asks Anatol.

"Harmless or poisonous," says Dombrowskaya, "either way, he could have waited until it wilted."

What Vladimir calls an *encounter:* three people at a low, round table, imitation Chippendale. The wife is listening to her husband while he is discussing a serious topic like drilling for oil in the Near East, or feeding mankind in the future from the bounty of the seas. She sees the growing animation in his eyes, hears his eager voice transforming dry words into ciphers, giving them an entirely new, different, strange, and threatening meaning. She turns her head slowly, millimeter by millimeter, struggling against her own resistance, she is afraid of what she will see because it is already there and can no longer be avoided: the merciless juggernaut, the monster. The other woman.

In one of Vladimir's pieces we all appear together, in single file like a Charleston-Revue, each of us with one hand on the shoulder of the chorus member in front, the other hand resting on our hips. We sing our parts individually:

NADINE:	I'd like a man who can talk to me,
CYRIL:	And a friend who'll do my taxes!
SANDRA:	And a gangster who won't hesitate
	To fill my loveless nights!
KAY:	I would love to laugh at the world outside.
AGATHA:	But a troubadour is what I need . . .
BOZENA:	And a little child to cradle,
VLADIMIR:	And a harlequin—
DOMBROWSKAYA:	And a wise old man:
	tender and gentle,
NADINE:	Ironlike . . .
PENNY:	For me a new Daddy!
SANDRA:	And a black man for me.

Afterward, Anatol appears in a top hat and tails in front of the footlights, pointing a kid-gloved finger at his chest, and in funereal tones he says:

"I, for my part, want nothing but my peace."

We applaud; this is one of the few of Vladimir's works that is accepted all around. No one feels especially misunderstood or unappreciated.

Vladimir has no biography; his life—and here we find similarities with Agatha, although he would never agree—consists of his stories, which he considers to be more real than all of the external events affecting our house. We don't want to argue, we leave him be. He may even be right.

The only self-portrait we have shows him in rags, run down, of indeterminate age, sitting on an embankment, blue frozen legs visible between tattered pants legs and shoes full of holes, reddish blue hands, too, resting loosely at his side, head leaning against a tree, relaxed, gazing cheerfully into the distance. The face of a victor: it has detached itself from his body, it carries him along serenely like a burden that is not worth the effort needed to throw it off, a transitory affront . . . Vladimir, this much is clear, knows himself to be in harmony with something, but he can't say what this something is.

Heavy flakes of snow are falling behind him on the pier. In the company of several brown leaves, the dog comes rolling across the street, diagonally, mechanically, one white ear, one black, the black ear standing up and crimped at the tip. We know this dog even though we have never seen him before: a little cylinder with a pyramid at the front, brown monocle on his right eye, ear tipped over—a clown of a dog. Not until he is sitting next to Vladimir, nonchalantly gazing into the distance, does the relationship become clear: he is the abandoned brother, a piece of Vladimir, a piece of us.

Nadine's attempts at escape are the inspiration for Vladimir's silent-film scene called "Rescue." At first all we see is a nighttime street in the suburbs, a man is walking along accompanied by a few bursts of melody from an ocarina. He is obviously tired of living; we see him walking through puddles giving no heed to his shoes. At this moment, Nadine bolts out of a nighttime house in the suburbs, her hair disheveled and screaming loudly for help. Behind her, rushing out of the same house, the evildoer, Cyril, with a mustache and a mouth full of curses, is brandishing a weapon we immediately recognize to be Dombrowskaya's cigarette holder.

"Help!" is the title of the scene, and refers, of course, to Nadine's screams, while her heels fire a salvo of shots onto the pavement, which in the neighbors' dreams may be either a fireworks display or an execution, each according to his own temperament, but it still does not have the power to bring the raging Cyril to a halt.

The stranger has this power. Mid-puddle he interrupts his stride and simply waits until Nadine reaches him and, sobbing freely, throws her arms around his neck as well as his entire shrunken person. Only then does he turn his eyes to Cyril, who, mustache, weapon, and unspeakable curses at the sight of this new set of circumstances, decreases his speed, comes to a stop, contemplates, and finally initiates a threatening retreat from the nighttime suburban street back into the nighttime suburban house.

The sobbing Nadine and her rescuer suddenly find themselves in the middle of an emptiness populated solely by the eyes of neighbors who, finally awake, search the street for the source of their dreams, execution or fireworks, accordingly. To their disappointment they espy nothing more than two embracing figures who must appear to them to be the usual pair of lovers, no reason for dreams. Surly, they pull their heads back in.

We see the pair once more, close up; they seem to have reversed their roles: the rescuer has become a new man, suddenly he's interested in living again, and leaving no doubt about how things stand, he even takes his feet out of the puddle. Nadine, on the other hand, is still sobbing. A title appears: "Which one has been rescued?" Immediately after this, all we see is the abandoned street in the suburbs, with the likewise abandoned puddle, as well as a text that makes our eyes ache: "Save me, then I'll save you . . . Let me save you and I'll be saved . . . Save me, whoever can . . . " "Etc." at the end.

A word in support of Agatha. She may be dumb. She may be sentimental and so proper that we are embarrassed to recognize her as one of us, not to speak of allowing her out of the house—but one thing we cannot deny: when nothing else helps, she comes to our rescue. When Anatol can no longer stand this life, when the dissension in our house robs us of our peace, or when, as now, Nadine, in her recklessness, exposes us to incalculable danger, a brief respite in Agatha's world of pictures allows us to forget both danger and sadness.

In this sense she also created the picture of Jeremy's house, especially the color: a muddy dark lilac, washed out, peeling, beneath a slate roof that also has a slight lilac tint. Against the side of the house, between the windows, there is a large shrub in a very definite deep green, which provides the finishing touch to this decaying house: a lilac bush.

"Clever," says Cyril.

"Are you certain," asks Vladimir, "that its blossoms are lavender and not white?" Agatha is certain, the harmony is retained. Nevertheless, she is unable to prevent discord: Jeremy steps out of the house, Jeremy's mother steps out of house, both have red hair, Agatha's harmony is shattered, the dissonance becomes obvious, something is crying for resolution, accord.

"Let's stay on track," says Cyril.

The house belongs to the old man, everything here belongs lock, stock, and barrel to the old man although he doesn't seem to be particularly interested in his possessions, not in the inn, not in the land, not in his wife who reads books. If he cares about anything, it would have to be the trout stream and fishing. And what about little Jeremy who grew up in his care? A blade of grass in the care of a steamroller, says Cyril. He wasn't even two years old when his father pointed a finger at him and said:

"One day he'll be reading books, too, I can see it now." Anyone who knew the old man knew what he meant.

The inn was called Pleasant View, although from there you could see nothing more than a stream in a narrow valley and cowslips in spring, marsh marigolds in summer, red beech trees in autumn, after that nothing but mist. The nearest village was three kilometers away, the nearest city thirteen kilometers; here you were on your own. Your own! In summer the inn was flooded with tourists, they sat at tables under umbrellas from morning until late in the evening, some stayed overnight in order to go hiking the next day, all of them stolid people, families with children, young married couples, sometimes even elderly teachers with sensible shoes. The Pleasant View was a gold mine from spring to autumn.

Assuming that the summer wasn't a rainy one—because here everything depended on the weather: shopping, menus, the number of waitresses, everything was organized around the weather. Jeremy, says Cyril, saw more of the weather in his first ten years than most people see in seven times that. No wonder he was so tired of it! He preferred the harsher seasons, when the weather was not of much importance, only customer traffic.

The old man had remodeled the guest rooms immediately after monetary reform, his wife kept her amazement to herself, and she didn't ask any questions; what went on in this house was solely his business, she was responsible for the kitchen and for Jeremy's upbringing, that was all, and he didn't interfere in these matters. It wasn't until he had a new heating system installed that she understood he was planning for winter guests, and this surprised her all the more: the Pleasant View was pure purgatory in winter. But there she was mistaken: guests came, if never for very long, some arrived in the middle of the night and left before breakfast, so that they never even had a chance to note the absence of a view, let alone a pleasant one, and no one complained. They seemed to pay well; the old man traded in his rattletrap delivery truck for a new and bigger one, he had the restaurant paneled with pine. And he wasn't stingy with his family either: any wish his wife might have, she could fulfill, but she didn't wish for much; she would liked to have traveled, but that wasn't possible because of her responsibilities in the kitchen.

Once she stopped being surprised about the curious winter guests—this took quite some time, for she was a teacher's daughter from the village and had no perspective regarding such things—she took Jeremy to a boarding school and only brought him back home for the summer holidays when the lively business of the day could at least obscure the aberrations of the night. Fortunately, Jeremy, like his mother, had the habit of getting up early and going to bed early; in the evening the old man took care of the business on his own.

Fishing was the only activity shared between father and son; in the midday heat, along the trout stream, Jeremy became acquainted with another man, a man who was dissatisfied with his innkeeper's life, who found it difficult to hold his restlessness inside, and used the mute hours at the water to lay things out for himself: perhaps a way, or a solution, maybe even an escape. Still, it amazed him that his father raised no objection when Jeremy revealed his plans to study archeology rather than training to become an innkeeper. He seemed to be as unconcerned about the future of the Pleasant View as he was about the future of his son.

"There's something wrong here," Jeremy said to his mother.

"I am the wrong wife for him," she said.

"I am the wrong son," said Jeremy. They looked at each other, both with this indeterminate eye color, both with unusually pale pigmentation over a scaffolding of bones as delicate as a bird's . . . Neither one of them was more than a fistful for the old man, says Cyril, he could easily have squeezed them into a puree, if he had wanted to . . .

By the time he might have wanted to, Jeremy had already been studying for six semesters. He went directly home at the beginning of the holidays, by train to the city, by bus to the village. There, on the dusty square in front of the post office, stood the old man's delivery truck. Jeremy opened the back door and threw in his suitcase; then he went up to the front seat.

It must have been very hot; the bus was still standing there, the driver had gotten out and was leaning against the

running board on the shady side, rubbing away with his handkerchief at the red streak left behind on his forehead by his
cap. A boy rode by on his scooter carrying a clanking milk
can. Under the awning of The Post House a peasant of a waitress was noisily dragging chairs back into place.

Over her folded arms, Bibi had laid her head on the steering wheel. She winked at Jeremy out of one eye.

"Well, well," said Jeremy, "a new driver."

"I am the girl Friday here," said Bibi, and lifted her head.
"Get in, young man."

That was the beginning of everything, but still nothing
that would have awakened Sandra; she dozes on, leaving it to
Cyril to record events: the house was freshly painted, gone
the muddy lilacs, the new era was garnet red. In the entryway
it still smelled of Wiener schnitzel and cucumber salad, as it
always did at this time of the day in the summer, but his mother was no longer standing in the kitchen, she was lying in bed
in her room upstairs, the room that had formerly been his
parents' bedroom, a bedside table full of medicines announced her defeat, Jeremy knew everything even before he
saw and comprehended the old man, that this was no old
man but a man like himself, a man at the height of his powers who had found a reason for living.

All because of this wench, of course, she was nothing
more than that, she was one of those sort who came out from
the city with their men on winter evenings for a bottle of wine
and a short night, most of whom left again before breakfast,
and only one, Bibi, had stayed . . .

Now, everyone wants to know how this came about, even
Sandra is listening for the first time, but this is just the part
that is so difficult to report, because none of us was there, we
only know what Jeremy knows about Bibi, the purely superficial aspects. Vladimir claims that he can well imagine this
encounter, but he's precisely the one we don't want to entrust
with this matter, he would give us a grotesquerie, the man as
a faun, no doubt, and Bibi as a nymph, both entwined in

some ridiculous courtship dance, a parody of sensual powers and we're not interested: we appreciate Vladimir's distance, but not in all things.

Only Sandra can tell this story, but Sandra is not a practiced storyteller, she might be up to a little stage prompting, but that's all. Thus, we are introduced to what follows in catch phrases, lit by flashbulbs: the dining room of the Pleasant View on a winter evening, warmly paneled, warmly lit, a single couple holding hands, their heads pressed together, hydrogen peroxide and brilliantine, they are in a hurry to finish eating and will take a bottle of wine with them up to their room. The old man writes out the check, platter of cold cuts, wine, one night, two marks each for breakfast that will not be eaten. He goes back to the other side of the counter, turns the dial on the radio until he finds zither music, the old man has a weakness for zither music, while the man with the brilliantine whispers to his blond lady, charming her out of one giggle after another.

New guests: an engine is downshifted in order to make the turn into the Pleasant View, tires in slush, slamming doors and shoes on the mat in front of the door. The usual: a couple, in what is only a transitory alliance, cold cuts along with a glass of wine, a bottle up to the room. The old man suddenly realizes that he finds the man disgusting. This surprises him; it is the first time that he has looked at a guest critically. And he cannot see any purely superficial reason for his disgust: this man is a guest like many others, well nourished, with thinning hair, pudgy fingers, a lecherous grin.

The old man pours himself a schnapps before he goes to the table. He wants to throw the guy out, but he can't. He won't give him a room, then they'll have to leave, both of them. That's just it. He only wants the man to go, the girl should stay. The old man is confused, because there's nothing special about the girl either; she has a strong build, dark, her expression is not quite as fatuous as the blond's. Otherwise, nothing. Her companion appears to be boring her, she is playing with beer coasters, nodding now and then, she can't possibly be paying attention. The ass is talking about his deals. In furs. Maybe that's the bait.

He takes their orders; the guy wants a warm dinner, that's not possible, the kitchen is closed. Even this tiny snub gives the old man pleasure. If, however, the young lady would like something warm for dinner, then he, with his own hands, will sauté a cutlet or a steak, anything she'd like . . . The young lady has no such wish. She is building a house out of beer coasters. At this point she looks up and smiles at him, a smile of familiarity, as if they were old friends. But he knows for certain that he has never seen her before, and as he's going into the kitchen, his spine tingling from her smile, he also knows: he wants her.

"That's the point where lightning struck," says Vladimir.

"I don't understand it," says Cyril. "What was so special about her?"

"Something special enough to drive the old man crazy," says Nadine.

The old man is crazy. As he sets her dinner down in front of her, he is trembling, maybe for the first time in his life. He's not looking at her anymore, but her nearness makes it hard for him to breathe. Then he stands behind the counter for an eternity, leaning against the cabinet because his knees can no longer bear his weight, waiting. When the fur salesman leaves the room briefly, the old man takes action without thinking. He goes to the table and tells her that he could use a girl like her at the inn.

"For what?" Bibi asks. She understood immediately, he sees her thinking it over. That encourages him. "Send him away," he says and points with his head toward the door.

"I can't," says Bibi, "but tomorrow . . . " Between now and then there is a night he will not be able to endure. "And how will I get out of here?" The door opens and the man comes back.

"I'll take you wherever you want to go," says the innkeeper.

No one wants to describe this night that was five, or at most, six hours long, but like every other hell has no chronological boundaries.

"He repeated his entire life," says Cyril. "That can't be contained in couple of sentences, it would be a novel."

"It all depends on the morning," says Sandra. But Vladimir finds amusement in the details: the old man behind the couple on the steps, with one hand around the room key and the other clamped around the railing, murder in his heart, only a small scrap of reason holds him back—if he kills the guy he'll lose Bibi, too . . . Now he opens the door with difficulty and then, flat, as if crucified up against the posts, lets the two of them pass by . . .

"Would you like a wake-up call?"

"At five. Or is that too early?"

"That is not too early." Bibi grins. She wafts through the room, stops in front of the mirror, picks at her hair and waits for him to go. "I'll bring the wine," says the innkeeper.

More new tortures: downstairs, he is standing in front of the opened bottle wishing for a strong, fast-acting sleeping potion he could drop into the wine. But he doesn't have any. So he must serve them a love potion, which will free this miscreant of a fur salesman of his last inhibition, and Bibi of a justifiable sense of disgust . . . At this point he's perspiring. Standing at the door with the tray, he hears murmuring inside and would like to listen in, but the pounding of his heart in his ears drowns out the voices; he musters just enough strength to knock.

The man with pudgy fingers takes the tray, he has taken his jacket off and is wearing a hideous striped shirt; the old man looks past his fat arm into the room, and, in the room, he sees the curve of a bare shoulder, honey-colored in the light of the bedside lamp, a piece of shoulder is not much, but it will have to suffice, he takes it away with him like a talisman for this hellish night.

Bong, the clock in the dining room that strikes every quarter-hour, no living being can know how many quarter-hours a night like this night has, and the old man with his schnapps bottle, at the same table where Bibi sat with this lascivious old bastard, he isn't drinking much, he's just taking a swallow from time to time, he doesn't want to be drunk in the morning, he sits and counts, bong, bong, the quarter-hours.

"He repeated his life," says Cyril. "He searched the entire way for a point of reference for the renewal that was taking place inside, a renewal he had scarcely even sensed: not an old man, but a still-vital fifty, a man who no longer understood how he could occupy his abundant time doing nothing, and who suddenly felt alive, a wild man, and a fool."

"Nonsense," says Sandra, "that was only one of many quarter-hours." We know what she means: the long periods of despair, the murderous jealousy that drives him, bottle in hand, to steal upstairs, a horrible decision—to smash down the door and throttle that hideous monstrosity . . . But weakness held him back, he collapses on the landing, face down, the mounting for a brass rod across the red runner was all that was in his field of vision. He cries.

Actually we've had enough of the old man and his late spring, but we know how important this very scene is: it is the key to Jeremy's fate, and thus to his being, and thus to our experience; without this night in the Pleasant View, or so we believe, though this is idle speculation, there may have been no Bozena, no Sandra, maybe not even Dombrowskaya. And, for that reason—

"This has to be included," says Vladimir, "this macabre moment when he's lying there on the steps, no longer crying, having already surrendered, and suddenly hearing his name, and how he laboriously lifts his head and sees a few steps above him his wife in a long nightgown, even paler than usual in the glow of the blue nightlight, and how he struggles to remember: Who is this anyway? What does she want here? This," says Vladimir, "is exactly the way it was back then with Dombrowskaya when she saw Dombrowsky at the breakfast table, this feeling, that one must turn to someone else and ask, who could this be . . . "

"But only the morning counted." We find Sandra's tenacity unsettling; if we give in to her at this point then we'll be lost, at least for some time. Only after being worn away by her fantasies will we be able to find our way falteringly back to our own interests. Fortunately, Cyril is quick to act.

"Child's play, the morning," he says, "compared with the night! All he had to do in the morning was show the fur salesman out of the house—which gave him a great deal of pleasure; he could revel in the man's anger over this unexpectedly lonely departure—and needed only two turns of the key, one would have sufficed, but it was a symbolic act: once for this time and once for the entire future, and still he had enough time to turn out the lights in the dining room and climb the stairs again, step by step. At this point he was completely awake and totally rational. He didn't bother to knock on the door but went right in and just stood there; finally he took three steps straight ahead and fell down on one knee in front of the disheveled bed, still redolent of the loathsome salesman, but he didn't even seem to bother him anymore . . . And that's just how we'll leave him, on his knees in front of Bibi's bed, because this, basically speaking, was his ultimate posture, the one he was to hold until the end . . ."

"If that isn't frightening," says Anatol.

"The best is yet to come," says Sandra.

"Slaves," says Dombrowskaya, "are no compliment to a woman," and for the first time Sandra snaps back, saying:

"—but a pleasure."

Back then, when Jeremy told her this story, Sandra was not nearly so involved, she gave him to understand that she was a little bored. She lay next to him in the grass chewing on a single blade; from time to time she patted her lips with her fingertips to hide a small yawn.

"Do you believe he was a good lover?" she asked after a while. "As good a lover as you are?"

"A better one, very likely," said Jeremy, "otherwise she wouldn't have betrayed me with him." Sandra didn't immediately understand; her plantlike languor allowed for no immediate shock. Instead, she raised herself up onto her elbows, looked inquiringly into Jeremy's face, as if she expected a joke, and then asked:

"Betrayed in what way? Betrayed you? What did you have to do with her?"

"She was my wife," said Jeremy. "I married her the following year, not long after I had first seen her in our delivery truck on the square in front of the post office, you know, when she picked me up from the bus."

"I don't know anything," said Sandra, "anything at all." She sat up and rested her forehead on her knee; after that there was only the appearance of Sandra sitting in the meadow—in reality we were all there, or almost all, a confusing chaos: Bozena shaken with pity, over and over again, and Anatol, who kept moaning that he could no longer endure this life, not his own and not the life of the others, Nadine in between, horrified that such a thing could ever happen, Kay: Well, that's what you get, Bozena again, who suddenly understood everything, and finally Cyril, recording.

If it weren't for Cyril, Jeremy's story would have disappeared in the confusion.

During his semester break Jeremy saw everything, or so he thought: the new man his father had become, his mother's illness, all in all the more vigorous, younger life in the Pleasant View, and the reason for it all—Bibi. He considered himself an objective observer: the old man, he told himself, is in love with Bibi, the mother, unable to put up a struggle, has fled to the sanctuary of her medicines, Bibi herself enjoys her status in the house, her power over the old man, her independence. She is hardworking, the coffee has gotten better, the menu has broadened; her purchases lead to profits; there are no problems with the staff; she is a born innkeeper.

"Let's not fool ourselves," said the doctor as he left—they were standing on the landing and Jeremy was looking at the mounting for the brass rod across the red runner, the same one that had tormented the old man's eyes back then, but he didn't know that, of course—"your mother doesn't even want to get well. Nothing can be done for her. You'll have to see to it that the girl leaves, so that life regains its meaning for her."

"I'm not the head of this household," said Jeremy. "Talk to my father."

"I've already done that several times," said the doctor. He shrugged his shoulders and left.

Bibi wasn't coy; in her relationship with Jeremy she was uninhibited in a sisterly way. She approached him when he sat in the garden with his books, and listened to him talk about his studies. Sometimes they walked into town together, or they drove to the city to do the shopping. Once they went dancing; Jeremy was entranced.

"Now I'm beginning to understand my father," he said laughingly to Bibi. "Do you realize the old man is head over heels in love with you?"

"How can that be? Why would he leave us alone like this?"

"He's just being clever," said Jeremy. "He knows that he doesn't have a chance." And Bibi laid her head on his shoulder in such a way that he couldn't see her face.

His mother was getting worse, and one of her relatives moved into the Pleasant View to take care of her, as they say, but in reality she was there to get to the bottom of all those rumors. The deciding scene was not long in coming. Jeremy, walking along the corridor on a rainy morning with a book under his arm, heard the strangely cramped laugh of the old man coming from the restaurant.

"You're barking up the wrong tree," he said. "You'll have to talk to my son. If I'm not mistaken"—Jeremy opened the door, and the old man looked him in the face and said—"he's well on his way to marrying Bibi."

"Me—of course," said Jeremy, "it's only a question of setting a date."

"From then on," says Cyril, but Vladimir, who had been silent up until now, interrupts him mid-sentence:

" . . . fishing was not the only thing father and son had in common."

"Oh, hell," says Kay.

" . . . from then on there was no way to stop things," Cyril says, completing his thought.

"What, for example?" asks Nadine, but suddenly Cyril no longer seems to be listening; he is holding his story on his knees and begins wildly leafing through it, counting pages, miscounting, beginning to count all over again:

"For God's sake," he says, "not another word about Jeremy. He is already taking up twice as much space as he was allotted, he's going to ruin my whole story!" He runs his hand through his hair and continues carrying on to himself. "A secondary character, nothing but a secondary character, I shouldn't have allowed this . . . "

"It doesn't make any difference now," says Nadine. "I'd like to know what happens."

"Imagine it for yourself," says Cyril. This rudeness brings Dombrowskaya into the fray.

"You are forgetting," she says, "that we're not holding this discussion to help you with your story, but to keep Nadine from carrying through with her, ahh, intentions. So let's get on with it, and you can make it short."

The two of them spent their honeymoon in Jeremy's student quarters, six tender weeks without any major commotion. Then Bibi became restive and Jeremy understood.

"In three semesters," he said, "I'll be finished and we can get an apartment." In the meantime, Bibi moved back into the Pleasant View. For a year they kept up a long-distance marriage; then his mother died and Jeremy went back home. It was a snowless winter, nothing but mud and fog. The delivery truck stood on the square in front of the post office.

"A crying shame about this scene," says Vladimir. "It's worth an entire chapter, and what are you making of it? You're giving away the best things!"

"Not now," says Cyril, "some other time!"

Jeremy threw his suitcase into the back of the truck and walked up to the front. The old man was sitting behind the wheel, a strange sight in his black suit, numbed, pale, beaten.

"It's come to this," he said, instead of a greeting. "I wasn't able to help her. I wasn't able to help myself." Jeremy wanted to squeeze his father's hand but he had already turned his attentions to the ignition. "She will have to forgive me," he said.

Once they were out of the village and the shingled roof of the Pleasant View could be seen through the trees, he asked:

"You heard what I said? That I couldn't help myself?"

"Yes, Father."

"And you will have to forgive me, too," said the old man.

What comes now is simply this one afternoon after the burial: Jeremy in his mother's room, looking at papers, filing. The old man on a chair in the corner, his hands covering his face, breathing heavily. Then both of them in the doorway to the dining room: they are looking at Bibi, who is sitting at a table in a garishly flowered dress and building a house out of beer coasters, which keeps falling down, apparently because she's drunk.

At first she laughs, and that's bearable, but then she starts talking and that's bad, although what comes out is nothing but the unblemished truth, assuming that the word *unblemished* can be used in this context; she doesn't hold anything back. Jeremy meets the whore Bibi. By the time he leaves, he has also found out everything else, even this business with the fur salesman, even with his own marriage . . . Everything is confirmed by a glance at the old man who is standing next to the bar, head hanging down on his chest, an accused man admitting his guilt . . .

And that's it, the story has taken its course, Jeremy's future has been determined: the escape into his studies, which, fortunately, dealing solely with the past, spares him the present; his fear of people because people can wound; his lies. And what's already there: the encounter with us, Nadine, Bozena, Sandra; the end.

"He'll be back," says Sandra.

"He never really left," says Bozena.

"It's about time you forgot him," says Nadine.

Penny, interested in fathers as she is, barges in with questions about the old man's well-being.

"It's just not true that they're both dead," she says. "Only Bibi's dead. But Cyril wants him gone so he can have a better ending, Cyril blows people away whenever he feels like it. If I did anything like that . . . "

Cyril relents. Okay, okay, the old man's alive; he is sitting in the Pleasant View slowly wasting away together with his business, he is no longer very involved. Most of the time he can be found at the stream, fishing, with God knows what on his mind. He has no injuries from the accident, no external ones at any rate.

"I don't want to argue about the truth," says Cyril, "but the other version would be more convincing: the old man and Bibi in the delivery truck on the square in front of the post office. It's drizzling. They have just picked up the registered letter from Jeremy's lawyer, the one with the divorce papers. Bibi is folding the pages together. 'Well, so what,' she says, 'maybe it's all for the best. What do you think,' she asks, 'say something, will you!' The old man turns his attention to the ignition. 'He'll have to forgive me,' he says. After that there's only the wet road, the fog and a curve beyond the village where many things have come to pass. And Jeremy again, in an empty house, a macabre repetition: busy with papers, organizing assets . . . "

"It's lucky life isn't this melodramatic," says Kay.

"Do you have any idea!" says Cyril.

Nadine is losing her patience. This Jeremy had already cost her too much time and emotional energy, and whatever, and, when it comes right down to it, her entire bourgeois existence . . . although he had been Bozena's and Sandra's affair, by God, not hers . . . And so on, we've heard this all before; we don't really bother to listen anymore.

Bad enough that Jeremy still meant so much to everyone else, but Cyril's annoying habit of working out possibilities was making this whole thing unbearable . . .

"If we all started saying 'if'! We can't even imagine the ramifications! If I had not married Dombrowsky back then, but someone else . . . If Bozena had made an appearance at Dombrowsky's instead of Jeremy's . . . If Kay hadn't taken a job at the newspaper but had gone to America with Viola . . . " *She* shouldn't have said this.

"Impossible to imagine?" asks Kay. "I've been imagining this for a long time. Things would have been *like this*—"

"Some other time," says Nadine, "not now."

"Yes, now," says Kay, "now."

Nadine presses her hands against her temples; there's nothing else she can do.

Kay, who forces us to back up and go in another direction, taking a detour we would like to have avoided because it seems superfluous to us, and brings us to the theme *opportunities lost*, a theme that is unsatisfying, unedifying, inexhaustible . . . Only Dombrowskaya is curious: "Let her talk, I would like to know how things are going to turn out." This is how they turn out:

Kay, who, in a definite place (squeezed in between a cot and a wardrobe), at a precise moment (postwar November, three o'clock in the afternoon), to an explicit question (yes or no?), answered "yes" instead of "no."

The lieutenant smiled; to this extent, nothing had changed. Only the sigh finishing off his smile was new.

"My goodness," said the lieutenant, "now we're really going to get into a paper war." The engagement kiss is forgotten. Instead he asked for her papers.

"Which ones do you mean, my birth certificate or—"

"Everything you've got, every scrap you can find, no matter what's on it, including a copy, if possible!"

It was only when he was standing in the doorway that he seemed to notice her again, how she, squeezed in between bed and wardrobe, was biting her nails and watching him.

"Not at all like a bride," he said, "more like an animal in a trap." He jumped over a chair, stepped into a suitcase, and kissed Kay on the forehead. "I'm very kind to animals," he said, "and I detest brides."

He was very kind to her, brought her things that delighted her, a bolt of red silk for a dress—"maybe you'll look like
a woman in it, you never know"—shoes, and a nightgown
made of nylon: "It's just the usual kind of thing," he said, "you
shouldn't let it frighten you."

He complained to her about Jutta's lack of understanding:

"She doesn't want to admit that with me she would be the
unhappiest woman alive. It wouldn't even take three weeks, I
tell her, and you would leave me! An itinerant actor! A man
without furniture! Without a home! But no—she only sees
this, here"—he taps himself on his shoulder bars—"and what
she calls opportunities for advancement: the army will give
you a job, she says, the army will pay for your education!
Mama mia! And I say to her: what you need is a career officer,
advancement built into the plan . . . "

"Maybe she loves you," said Kay.

"Oh no, not that, never that," said the lieutenant.

Kay as a bride, and later the young wife of a very good-
looking American officer of Italian descent; people are surprised. Short hair, long pants, bangs; opening her eyes, biting
her nails: she is well aware of her lack of femininity, but circumstances keep her from recognizing her shortcomings as
shortcomings. Jutta is a woman with all the attendant means,
and Jutta has lost. Kay feels neither jealousy nor triumph,
actually this involuntary victory seems more of a burden than
anything else, she would like to go to Jutta and ask her for-
giveness, but Jutta wants nothing to do with her.

And so they are married, at headquarters, with two offi-
cers as witnesses, Kay in a gabardine suit and in her hand a
bouquet of carnations that she holds like a tennis racket.
They eat turkey in the casino, and the lieutenant squeezes
her little finger and whispers: "Wake up! This is supposed to
be one of those great moments! A turkey for life!"

"For life" was a new phrase, she hadn't heard it used since

her Latin classes, *non scholae . . .* , and even then she hadn't taken it seriously, nor did Viola take it seriously, she could see that, but there was still one question: for life; did that mean for a long time? forever? entirely? She studied Viola's profile, he was handsome, not only elegant, not only good-looking, but handsome like a Roman. His parents had also been handsome, "until they died," he had said, "which is not very difficult if you die young." In the picture they were standing by a fence which enclosed a charming little house that wasn't theirs. "A trick of my father's," said Viola. "He loved tricks; they had never had a house and didn't want one. Traveling folk," he said, "vagrants. Like you and me."

The uniform looked so good on him. Don't be blinded by my uniform, he had said, it's just part of the act . . . She wasn't blinded, either by the uniform or the Roman profile. She had allowed him to choose her and take her away with him, nothing more. Ears of corn, pale stalks of celery, sweet notes flowed from the jukebox, notes meant for girlfriends not for wives: "A rose must remain with the sun and the rain . . . " and "I'll be loving you, always . . . "

They accepted everyone's good wishes and didn't know what to do with them.

"You should imagine that you're onstage," said Viola, "you stay in your role, that's all. That's what I do, things are easier that way. Afterward, after the curtain falls, you're yourself again." That was the hard part: she didn't know who she herself was.

A dreadful story, we all agree: how can such a child be allowed to marry? And, moreover, such an unfathomable sort as this Lieutenant Viola? A young girl, Bozena laments, who has seen nothing of life outside her carefully sheltered childhood . . . At this point the first protests come to life:

"Not much can happen to anyone coming out of Penny's school," and "Marriage is not the worst thing . . . ," and "He's not about to swallow her whole."

A child, Bozena continues, who hasn't got the slightest sense of her own person, who can't possibly know what resources she has within herself, what potential . . .

At this point, everyone is laughing. Bozena deserves what she's getting. Are we supposed to believe she had a real sense of herself back then, or even now?

But the story goes on:

Mrs. Viola on the deck of an ocean steamer in foggy weather, wrapped up like a mummy. Nothing has changed. The lieutenant has his arm around her shoulder, he is holding her like a bundle of fur and wool, he kisses her on her salty cheek and asks:

"Is it very much of a letdown to be married?"

"No, not at all, I wasn't expecting anything."

"Oh," he said, "I'm a lucky man!" She still doesn't know why he is laughing at her, but she notices that he's not unhappy and for her that will suffice.

"Are you expecting anything at all, my darling?" In response he gets a very vague bit of information: a gesture to the fog and a shrug of her shoulders.

"But I'm not bored," she said, as if apologizing.

A crossing in the fog, concealing the view where there is nothing to see, and in the middle between two continents, not yet disengaged here and not yet anchored there, Viola's new presence.

They danced the jitterbug in the cabin in matching pajamas because she was afraid of the nightgown, and Viola was so exuberant that he finally danced by himself, legs like rubber, dynamically dislocated . . . In the end he took her by the hand and bowed with her: "The Viola Brothers have been honored!" and they laughed until they were out of breath. A little later he stuck his head out from the upper bunk and said:

"I should have adopted you; then I'd still be able to marry a blond."

"But why, when you've got me." She was ready for anything, obedient.

"I feel like an idiot," said Viola, "but I may get over it."

"Tell me about how people feel," she said, "I mean, when they sleep together. It's really nothing at all! And everyone makes such a fuss about it."

"That is because," said Viola solemnly, sitting on the edge of her bed and buttoning the top button of her pajamas, "there is something about it that makes people crazy, and something that you, in your angel-like transitional state, have not yet comprehended. Maybe, if you loved me . . . "

"Don't I love you?"

"A little, and a little differently."

"And you? Do you love me?"

"A little differently, too," said Viola, "but very much."

There was an apartment without furniture, as he had promised, that is, the furniture was for most part made of plastic, even the wardrobes and the dressers. Everything else, beds, tables, and chairs, was made of metal.

"Everything belongs to us," said Viola, "and everything together makes one carful; we are free."

Even as a civilian Viola was handsome, just in a more casual way, even in a hat and coat he still looked like a farm boy visiting the big city. He left every morning, he returned every evening tired but happy. "I only perform during the day," he said and expected no questions, so she didn't ask. Once she wanted to know where he was performing, in which part of the city, and she had a city map in hand so she could search out the site with her finger, but he wouldn't go into details.

"Everywhere, somewhere different all the time," he said, and she folded the map. She didn't want to bother him.

Still, she's very happy in New York. Viola gives her spending money, and he's almost no work, only breakfast and dinner, two rooms to keep clean, it's really child's play. During the day she wanders through the streets, a teenager with bangs and big eyes, she discovers the subway and the dime stores, and sometimes in the afternoons she goes to the movies, munching on popcorn and reclaiming the years of her youth, which had slipped away from her between school and the war, wonderful years, as she can see now, she hadn't imagined them this way.

People she meets, mostly young girls like herself, or older, motherly women, ask her where her parents live. She answers without correcting their misconception; she's leading a double life.

In the evenings she tells him about her adventures.

"It's remarkable," says Viola, "you're getting younger and younger. In Germany you still looked like a nineteen-year-old, but now you could be sixteen."

"Are you sorry," she asks, "that you married me?" No, of course not, how could he be sorry . . . "You," she asks suddenly, "why did you marry me, anyway? Tell me why!" At first he tries joking with her:

"For your money," he says, "because of your overpowering sensuality . . . Because of your immoderate love for me . . . " For the first time she notices his voice; his tone is bitter. She lowers her head. The dishes from dinner are still on the table, along with the ketchup bottle, beer glasses, white bread crumbs.

"I'm sorry," she says. She is really feeling very young now, too young for all of this, almost comical in this environment where she plays housewife, while at the same time feeling like a young child helping her mother with her work, but there is no mother and Viola is much too young to be a father, at most he could be her brother, the Viola Brothers are honored . . .

"*I'm* sorry," Viola says. Kay now regrets never having been his girlfriend: another stage she skipped over, like those years of her youth she is presently regaining. When will she regain the others? When the years of marriage she is now bypassing? When will the right time ever converge with the right time?

"I was very alone," says Viola. She has just noticed that the tone of his voice had changed; he's not joking anymore. He's standing at the window and looking into the street; brick houses, each with five steps leading up to the front door, and decorative railings all exactly alike, even the small maple trees on the other side of the street, they are still young and their trunks appear to be thinner than the supports they're tied to.

Once before, in just this way, he had stood with his back to her, in front of a window, hardly a year has passed. Outside there was barbed wire and OFF LIMITS seen from the back, STIMIL FFO. He is still alone.

"The way I live and like to live, I'm not fit for a normal, middle-class woman." She doesn't understand; is this supposed to be another joke? Not fit? A two-room apartment on a pretty street, money enough that it doesn't have to be discussed, and he's reliable too, home every night, and his handsome Roman looks—not fit? All the Juttas of the world would be overcome with desire . . .

" . . . and a bear," he says, "is not much company over the long haul."

"A bear?"

Her handsome Viola is not joking; he has a bear, a fairy tale of a bear, and he's been keeping it a secret. He has turned around and his arms are folded; he's looking at her.

"How large?" asks Kay.

"Taller than I am."

"Can he dance?"

"Of course," says Viola, "that's how we make our living." For one whole minute he stays put, waiting, searching her face. Kay bites her fingernails. The fact that he sits down shows that he's no longer afraid of anything, or not much at any rate.

"You see," he says, "with a profession like this it's just not possible to have a middle-class wife. The war was my chance," he says, "the flotsam. You."

"Oh," she says, "yes, yes, now I understand." She stands up and carries the dishes into the kitchenette.

"Can I go with you?"

"If you'd like." Of course she'd like. She is washing the dishes because she won't have time to do it early in the morning; he will take her along tomorrow and every day. Something new is beginning.

Viola has second thoughts.

"I don't know if you really understand: we are not respectable people. Curiosity and pity, we can't expect much more, not from the adults anyway. It's different with the children, they belong to us. If you can accept that . . . "

"Oh, easily," says Kay. None of this really matters to her; it's not the people she's concerned about, it's the bear.

"What's his name?"

"Jobo."

She gives a start.

"What's wrong?"

"Say it again."

"Jobo."

"My God," she says, "my God. You have never said *my* name that way."

Kay's first encounter with Jobo took place in semidarkness in the twilight of the barn which shelters Jobo and is permeated by a sweet-sharp smell, the only thing about Jobo that marks him as a predator, otherwise he's just a teddy bear, a giant toy.

"Oh," she says, "he's cute."

They look into each other's eyes, because they are the only recognizable objects in this twilight. Jobo's eyes are larger than Kay's but appear to be smaller because his head is larger, and her eyes appear large in her small face. Jobo is sitting up, sniffing.

"He likes you," says Viola.

"He likes her!" shouts Cyril and grabs his head with both hands. "He likes her! Shall I tell you what happens next? Jobo becomes Kay's playmate; a colorful dream opens up: the three of them wander through the squares, always on the periphery of the big city at a point where the last gas stations give way to greenery, surrounded by cheering children, rewarded by grown-ups, stared at by everyone . . . Viola playing the hurdy-gurdy, Jobo dancing, coquettishly and passionately as never before; he has been dancing this way since Kay joined them . . . And Kay, in blue jeans and a leather jacket with fringes, passes her hat around. She has gotten even younger. In her regression from a nineteen- to a sixteen-year-old she hasn't stopped, no, she's already reached a ten-year-old state, truly becoming Viola's daughter, and, if you please, along the way she has created a childhood that was never hers, she has become little Kay, not Penny . . . An impossible story."

Cyril is being unfair and we tell him so. He has no right to interfere with Kay's story, she is the one who should know. But Kay isn't even bothered, just thoughtful, and somewhat melancholy:

"Some of this is true," she says, "the way Jobo dances, for instance, and the neighborhood where the gas stations give way to greenery . . . " But this thing with the ten-year-old, we learn, isn't true: because Kay has not become younger, but actually older, or not really older, just different, that's it, different.

She now has her work: Jobo. Jobo's health, Jobo's beauty, Jobo's well-being. Never before has she taken so much interest in another living being, not even in herself. She is transformed: in the morning she jumps out of bed and cannot wait to get to Jobo, who, recognizing her step from afar, claws impatiently on the wooden walls . . . She mixes treats in with his feed, and when Viola combs him she is there stroking his paws, scratching his ears . . .

Soon he'll only accept his feed from Kay; with his paw he shoves away whatever Viola sets out in front of him. He's even started to balk when Viola has him on a lead, yet he follows

Kay like a puppy. When she claps her hands he dances, even without music. A bear in love.

Viola doesn't yet know what to make of this; at first he was exceedingly happy over this favorable course of events, but after a few weeks his joy had already begun to fade; he feels left out. If he was alone before, now he is doubly alone: he no longer has even Jobo.

When Kay suggests giving up the expensive apartment in the city and moving into the stall next to Jobo's box, a stall that could, with a few small changes, be transformed into a charming studio apartment, he turns mean for the first time and tells her that until now money has been his concern, at least the money, he says, at least that. Furthermore, she can move in next to Jobo, if that's what she wants, it wouldn't be a difficult move, a little lifting and basta.

"But I don't understand—"

"Oh, shut up!" He's yelling now. He slams the door shut and doesn't come home until morning.

When a man like Viola starts to get mean then his downfall is certain, it's the point at which all other modes of behavior have been proven ineffective. Yelling at Kay is admitting defeat. When he comes home in the early morning he is so mind-numbingly drunk that he mistakes Kay for an enemy and raises his hand against her, but then, recognizing his delusion, he falls sobbing onto his bed. Kay reacts like a wife: she takes off his shoes and covers him with a blanket, he is still wearing his coat; she bends over his face and recognizes his former grace in those alcohol-blurred features full of sadness.

For the first time, on this day, she tends Jobo alone. Combing is not as difficult as she had thought. She pauses now and then to tell Jobo, as gently as she can, about his master's sudden malady.

"But we'll forgive him, won't we, Jobo?" Jobo rocks back and forth on his hind legs and growls a little.

They are making a lot of money: everyone who sees the fragile girl next to the bear reaches instinctively for his wallet, just as before people had reached instinctively for their hearts, shocked and full of pity. Kay thanks them with a smile and Jobo plays the little man. The children jump with joy.

A wonderful day; but in the evening Jobo is locked in his stall and Kay must go back into the city. This is the first time she has ever felt constrained.

Viola is sitting at the table drinking; he has a gin bottle and a water glass in front of him. Empty beer cans are rolling around on the floor. He has probably been waiting all day; he thought she had simply gone out to feed Jobo and that she would come directly back. Now she comes in and puts the bag with the money on the table; Viola puts his glass down and reaches for the bag, he lets his hand rest there, as if he no longer had enough strength to pull it back; he looks up at Kay through bloodshot eyes and laughs, embarrassed, as if she had caught him lying.

"Lieutenant!" says Kay; it is the first time she has ever addressed him this way and she doesn't know herself why she's doing it. Maybe it is an attempt to bring back the time of his best role, the easy self-assurance, the flawless uniform. Or maybe she wants to make him aware of the distance between them, a distance that hasn't diminished at all since that room in the barracks, and the barbed wire. It is not a reproach but simply a sign.

Viola lets his head fall onto his left hand, his right hand is still resting on the money bag, and next to it are the bottle with the gin and the water glass, now he looks like a drunkard taking a final plunge into oblivion, all the while breathing haltingly, labored, Kay is standing next to him and watching as he sinks into a kind of black-curled misery, *traveling folk* she recalls, and she remembers a sentence he used to describe his parents: Everything has its own proportions; a life intensely lived, but short.

She takes care of everything, even those things that had

seemed all but incomprehensible before, things like taxes and the renewal of their actors' license. Viola accompanies her less and less often to Jobo's stall; most of the time he's already drunk when she returns in the evening, and in the morning he is unable to get up. Sometimes he looks like he's about to hit her, but she is on her guard; as soon as she sees the brutishness in his eyes she runs away. And she has gotten into the practice of opening the door very carefully when she returns, entering only after she has looked over the entire room. She believes that one day he will be standing behind the door with a club or a knife in his hand, lying in wait for her; his hate is obviously beginning to narrow down to this outcome.

But it doesn't come to pass. Before he can do anything to harm her he makes his mistake and attacks Jobo. Jobo cannot be attacked. In the morning Kay finds him sitting next to his master, restless, with an uncanny look, the knife is lying there and his paw is bleeding from a small wound, Viola's back is broken in several places . . . Kay has to call the owner of the barn as a witness, the police must come and confirm that Viola was not sober, and therefore Jobo's was a case of self-defense, not viciousness . . .

"You can see how tame he is," says Kay, and walks over to Jobo, who standing erect embraces her with both paws, a scene of incredible tenderness.

And thus it continues . . . Kay and Jobo on the country roads, on the periphery of big cities, they move almost every year, furniture made of plastic and aluminum in the car, Jobo's trailer, barred and locked, has a small window with a red-check curtain through which he can see Kay behind the wheel . . . Every few years, when their travels bring them back to New York, Kay takes a half-day off, covers her head with a dark-colored scarf, and goes to the cemetery to Viola's grave, which is located next to his parents' and is faultlessly groomed by the groundskeepers. She lays down a small wreath and tries to remember: who was he? the lieutenant, the brother, the drunkard, the enemy, the animal trainer? Kneeling with folded hands in front of the stone that bears his name, she spends a long time searching but she can't find him; it's just as it was back then, on the crossing, a salty fog in which he has hidden himself, a fog she tries to penetrate with her wide-open eyes, biting her nails . . .

"Damn," says Cyril, "she's worse than Penny . . . "

"It's my fault," says Dombrowskaya, "I shouldn't have encouraged her . . . "

"But she only wanted the best," says Bozena.

Sandra is dreaming about a bear.

This story has left us with a bad taste in our mouths; only Kay has remained unmoved, wide-eyed, passive.

"A nice little act of revenge," says Cyril, "that's what we've got here."

"I might have guessed," says Dombrowskaya, "an excess of innocence is always suspect."

"But it's *me* you're cursing," cries Penny. "I am the beast and the devil incarnate! When Kay does this kind of thing, no one says a word! She's allowed to do whatever she wants!" Now even Kay is starting to pay attention.

"What's wrong with you, anyway? Didn't you like it?" Her purity is frightening.

"No," says Cyril, "we didn't like it."

"I was only fantasizing: what would have happened, if . . . " She is candid. Her voice has a metallic edge, innocence streams from her eyes, "the innocence," says Vladimir, "of a freshly polished guillotine."

"There's nothing we can do," says Dombrowskaya, "only one thing will help: guilt, again and again until she catches on. It's a matter of time," she says, "it will happen quite naturally."

"Not to me," says Kay, "not to me."

Anatol has had a relapse, it is no wonder after all this

excitement, basically it's Nadine's fault, right now everything is Nadine's fault, but this is simply an observation meant to inform, we don't pass judgment here, we are not a court.

One sentence: " . . . what would have happened, if . . . "—a sentence like this is enough to pull the rug out from under Anatol's feet. The abyss opens up for him and thus for us as well; we should have watched him more closely; we had forgotten him.

He is pacing back and forth in the room; we know this vigorous movement, a strong engine drives him, no one can stop him now, we will have to wait until he runs out of fuel and we never know how much he has.

" . . . what would have happened, if . . . ," says Anatol. "Let us assume for once: if Penny had been one meter taller? that meter she was missing? Assume just once . . . " He stops and hits himself on the forehead. "Murder and mayhem," he says and starts pacing again, "no, no mayhem, just murder. She would have razed her entire environs, diminished humanity."

"So what!" yells Penny, interrupting him. "So what, whose loss?"

"And Kay," says Anatol, "even worse: purity itself, heart full of ideals, and boom"—he slashes at his throat with the edge of his hand—"the sin is punished. The lieutenant's sin: that he hadn't seen her as a woman. Do you understand what I'm saying? This outcome was a possibility from the first moment on. What was she looking at in that room in the barracks when she tried to capture the lieutenant's attention by spouting all that anxiety, because she, scrawny, flat, and pole-legged as she was, hadn't been able to succeed in any other way. She was looking at the barbed wire, how it ran across the lieutenant's throat: his death was a foregone conclusion."

"That's not true," says Kay, "that's not true." Now we're really afraid: if no one manages to stop him, Anatol will drag us all down. Vladimir? But he only wants to know what's going to happen next. Not even Dombrowskaya is ready to help; she shrugs her shoulders and opens her palms, powerless. We hope that Anatol's motor will run down, that he'll get tired.

"... would have happened, if," says Anatol. "If Cyril had gotten a job at the newspaper two or three years earlier, that is, not *after* the war but *during* the war? Cyril with his ambition, his obsession with work, determined to serve the ideals taken over from Kay, the good, the true, the beautiful, and prepared to blindly accept them wherever they turned up, and how: the dream of a master race, for example, a Nordic mythology . . . What a monster he would have become," says Anatol, "one with a noble brow and the look of a prophet . . . if it weren't for those two, three little years . . . "

This is too much. We are benumbed. Cyril has turned white, he's not even searching for words; he has nothing to offer in opposition. This is unbearable. Why, for God's sake, do we have to put up with a curse like Anatol? We don't deserve it.

It has become so dark here that we don't even dare to hope for light. Nadine feels around in the cupboard for a bottle of raspberry brandy that has always been there, we don't consider this our salvation but still we hope she finds it, and above all, that it will do us some good. This is what's become of us, such a sad bunch, so utterly lost.

The bottle isn't there anymore and we won't be conducting an investigation to find out who's taken it, most likely Bozena has given it to some needy person, that would be just like her. We are thankful for this minor diversion, no one has dared to continue with Anatol's thoughts. Finally, Dombrowskaya does:

"And then," she says, "let's have it! Anatol is next in line. What would have happened if that afternoon had not come to pass, with the raindrop on the twig and the gaze through the coffeehouse window . . . " Anatol stops and studies the toes of his shoes; we can all see the table with the coffee cup and the glass of water, the newspaper, blood dripping slowly out of it—an extreme situation, a boundary. If not—

"Anatol," says Dombrowskaya, "with his permeable skin, his antennae vibrating around him from head to toe like a branch of asparagus, with his tendency to search for guilt even where there is none, calling it down upon himself until he collapses . . . Anatol, who views every dead person as his victim, and whose newspapers all bleed . . . What would have happened . . . "

"Madhouse," says Anatol.

We breathe a sigh of relief; he has understood. He will leave us in peace, for a while in any case. Living with Anatol has never been easy.

Anatol. The morning on which he awoke endangered, simply because of the fact that it was morning, this morning was possessed of extraordinary possibilities, he knew it, while glimmering phrases floated through his mind like *snowflakes in April* and *Perrier Jouet*.

He was lying on his right ear listening to the ticking of his pulse: a block of wood and there's a worm in it; tunneling and hammering, but where? He didn't know where his boundaries lay. If he doesn't move he'll never know what shape he has, he will remain an amorphous mass forever, with very few characteristics: dark, warm, content. And already a hope is escaping through this gap in his consciousness: as long as he didn't move anything was possible, any form, and any capability appropriate to it. He could be a block of wood, a cliff, a mountain. Everything which, because it is already dead, cannot be killed. Or, if it must be a living thing, then an animal with a talent for escape, a mole that disappears under the ground, a bird as light as a feather . . . In the most extreme case, an animal that doesn't have to retreat because it is armored, something like a crocodile with a back made out of handbags, covering a belly full of undigested clothing . . .

This image, unquestionably Nadine's influence at work, gave him a start—and with that he had moved, and now he suddenly knew where his boundaries lay; he again sensed a body like the body of a human being, legs, arms, a head pressed sideways into a pillow and much too heavy, and above all the agonizing inability to fly away, to disappear under the ground, to withdraw into a shell: he had only a silky thin skin, the clothing in his belly was from meals long past, of which he hadn't partaken—others might feast but he would be destroyed by doing so.

In a last attempt at escape, in spite of all the hostile circumstances, Anatol recalled the first words of the morning, *snowflakes in April* and *Perrier Jouet,* and added willfully: *lambswool, Rimini.* It didn't help, it was already too late. He gave up, opened his eyes, let his darkness be flooded with light and understood.

"Death," said Anatol, "this day; I will die." Just as he knew: this is a new day, now he also knew: this is my last day.

He was neither sad nor shocked, the only thing he felt was a faint sense of amazement: look here, your time is up, just add a fleeting sense of alienation; it was so simple: where was his instinct for survival? Somewhat embarrassed, he took his acquiescence to be a sign of his lack of vitality.

He was more attentive than otherwise to grooming, hot shower, cold shower, he wiped the steam from his mirror, he began to feel some regret about his body, which he had never paid much attention to: it looked to him to be a capable body and also well-formed, an auspicious incarnation, all in all, and, ultimately, you never knew if you would be as lucky the next time around—too bad about that. On the other hand, simply throwing a piece of bread away into the garbage distressed him, he had been brought up that way. What was it that his grandmama had said standing at her husband's coffin? It is a shame to bury a man with such good teeth . . . Of course she was a vigorous woman and liked to exaggerate.

Otherwise he had no complaints; he had, as he now admitted to himself, long been weary of the endless repetition, the requisite maintenance: cleaning, feeding and sleep, even breathing, he might change the sequence and the soap, but he was not permitted a break. He was not granted even two minutes of freedom. For him, it had sufficed.

Standing in front of the mirror he parted his hair and for

a moment he wavered about whether or not to finish off the part: Was it still worth it? His hair would have to be combed again anyway. Then discipline won out, behind which ingrained habit may be assumed, and he finished off his part, straighter and more narrow than any part he had ever made before, perhaps because it was to be his last.

Breakfast tasted the way it always had; he recalled past anxieties and they now seemed meaningless, even childish. Fear of death is something for pessimists: the odds stood at one to one. The greatest danger of all, the danger of death, was gone. Fear, Anatol told himself, while beheading his last soft-boiled egg, thrives on distance, embrace it and it loses its power. A spear, he said to himself, chewing in contemplation, which is useless in hand-to-hand combat . . . An echo without space . . . These images displeased him; there must be a metaphor that would correspond precisely to this case; resigned, he admitted to himself that he would hardly have time to find it.

Mrs. Mayer came into the room and asked if he'd like some breakfast rolls. He studied her eager face, her bluish hands; she was the way she always was, she hadn't noticed anything. Of course she would cry when she found out; Mrs. Mayer liked to cry and often did.

Accounting and departure, there was nothing more left for him to do. What had he achieved and what had he lost? Magically, everything seemed to square: blinders lost—vista won; trust sacrificed—certainty attained; and so on, the sum remained constant, only the details changed, happiness, for example. When had he been happy, where and with whom? Or without whom? He combed through his memories, subtracted the unhappy times, sorted the rest according to neutrality and fire, found: the answer wouldn't be found this way. Maybe this moment was happiness: fright behind him, fright awaiting him, the present suspended in honey—what honey this must be.

He won't bother with a farewell letter; neither words nor

addressees came to mind. Why bid farewell? It now seemed to him that since birth he had been doing nothing else.

He took his hat and left the house; this forenoon could do him no harm, on the contrary, he suddenly discovered choreographic lines in the easy movements of the pedestrians on both sides of the square, lines that led to two women with shopping bags, who were walking down the middle under the trees; the morning ballet. Anatol wondered how many times he had already missed this performance. Maybe the entire city was full of figures like these? Anatol walked faster; his time was short, he knew that, and there was still a lot he wanted to see; it suddenly seemed important to him to take the most meaningful impression of this world he possibly could with him into the next.

Things seemed almost too easy: at this point, life appeared to be so infinitely difficult compared with this unburdened exit. A step off to the side, nothing more than that. The powers that had been arrayed against him, for as long as he had been a sentient being, defending against them had taken up almost all of his energies, these powers were now tilting at emptiness. He tried in vain to recall problems that only days ago had been a burden; they had already been resolved. The question of his potential, for example, was no longer a question. He was content.

His gait was irregular, almost a limp; he pushed off with each step as if he intended to fly, but this never worked, he gave up and sank back to earth; still, he tried it again with the next step he took, and the step after that, too. He had, of course, always walked this way, but until this morning he had never noticed; he had a role in the ballet, he just didn't know which one.

A few steps later, a greengrocer caught his attention, a greengrocer with no vegetables in the boxes in front of the display window, only a blackboard with a message written in chalk: Lettuce inside because of the cold. At first Anatol thought he recognized the writing, then he realized the message had simply been printed, and that it must be something else. He stopped and thought; the blackboard reminded him of a gravestone; he squinted until the writing dissolved and then imagined his own name on the board: Anatol in the great beyond because of death. He didn't like this *beyond* so he tried other, different words: . . . absent because of death, and . . . somewhere else because of death. Finally he went into the store to assure himself that the message on the black-board was not just an empty promise. The sight of lettuce piled high on a table inside filled him with a thankfulness, so great that even he could see it was somewhat out of propor-tion. He bought three heads for sixty pfennig each and allowed the storekeeper's wife to show him their *firm and ten-der hearts.*

Back out on the street, he saw there had been an accident at the corner. Without curiosity, and in no hurry, he went closer; an ambulance left the square screaming, red lights flashing. People crowded around a streetcar that had stopped along an open stretch of track. As Anatol approached them he felt the undertow and let himself be swallowed up. A brief-case hit him in the side, the brim of a woman's hat touched his ear, he lost himself and for an indeterminate while he was nothing more than a piece of matter suspended in space.

Already, as the crowd was exhaling him again, he knew that the day had lost its danger. He had been rejected and someone else chosen. He thought about the ambulance and the red lights: that someone else was not happy, he was a vic-tim. Anatol had caused his death.

The shock took his breath away for some seconds, during which time he felt his arms and legs die away: just one more moment and the conditions of the morning would have been reinstated, these no longer desirable conditions which had held infinite promise of everything from being a block of wood to experiencing his own death, everything but this one possible outcome, the worst possible outcome of all.

Confused and stunned he hurried home, a man overcome by a calamity he cannot yet accept: one-half hour ago, hadn't it been impossible even to imagine that something like this could happen? And what difference can half an hour make, anyway—go thirty minutes back, and life was again what it had been, an innocent life though a threatened one, the tooth one never noticed before the pain began . . .

Abashed, he again found himself a captive of the everyday: the blackboard in front of the greengrocer had only one purpose, to point customers in the direction of certain goods; the pedestrians on the square had no intention of attuning themselves to a higher choreography, they obeyed the more earthly laws of the forenoon, a time of day dedicated to the acquisition and preparation of foodstuffs . . .

A man walking in front of him suddenly turned around, as if Anatol's gaze had sent a blow crashing in between his shoulder blades; he stopped, wavered for a moment, and then walked away with a big, hurried stride. Anatol turned around too, and discovered, to his relief, the face of a standard clock at his back: the man had been checking the time and noticed that it was later than he had thought. But this solace, too, was immediately torn away from him: a young woman dashed out of the front door of an apartment building, shot a lightning-fast glance in Anatol's direction, and raced away. At the same time he noticed others fleeing, a boy in a hooded coat tugging at his mother's hand, an old woman holding her hat tightly on her head and tripping along . . . The crowd grew. Anatol saw nothing but backs and fleeing feet, everyone rushing away ahead of him, he was involuntarily driving the herd before him.

He followed them because he found it impossible to stand still or to take another way; he went right past his own front door. He soon gave up his attempt to pass the others and to convince them of the futility of their flight; there were too many, and even if he had succeeded in catching up with the whole crowd and convincing them of his good intentions, it wouldn't have changed anything. Who cares about the intentions of a black cat who walks across the street from left to right on a Friday? He was an evil omen; he brought death.

The pursuit came to its unexpected conclusion in front of a movie theater in whose lobby a colossal placard promised a Rescue in the Night, Product Demo. Win One of Fifty Cameras. Anatol saw his herd disappear into the darkness in search of a salvation he believed to be a cheap sham since it was obviously associated with commerce. He waved off the doorman inviting him to come on in, and quickly walked away, staring down at the ground.

Anatol on the way back home: the city is entirely new. Lots of people, wide streets, and there, where he lived, a square like a stage set laid out in perspective, huge, paved with hewn stone . . . Scattered about here and there, nature. There stood a tree, right? Anatol walked up to the tree and touched its bark, took a step back and looked at its crown, didn't say a word: they had nothing to say to each other.

He decided to get something to eat. At his usual table in a pub near a railroad embankment, he tried to get his bearings, to untangle the impressions that had wound up into a knotted ball in his consciousness. The waitress's question gave him a start; every word was a dart, every dart seemed to hit the bull's-eye, in chaos any point might be the center. Whoever might want to encounter him at his usual table in his pub on the edge of town would encounter him. He wanted to escape.

His meal: he kept forgetting to tell her, so she always brought him a rare steak, he could already see it as she set it down on the table, it was too light for a thick steak, it couldn't possibly be done. He pressed it with his fork, it sprang back, he cut it, blood ran out of it, the plate turned red, the rice turned red. Anatol put his money on the table and left.

He made a detour: along the tracks on a path only as wide as his foot, heading toward a suburban train he could see coming his way. He loved this stretch of ground between the weeds and the metal, the city at his back, and next to him low-hung wires carrying low-voltage electricity. In his extremities he began to feel fatigue that allowed for no pain: walking along toward the suburban train, he knew it was easy to die, and thus easy to live. He walked leaning slightly to one side, leaning, by the weight of one shoulder, more toward death than life, but one shoulder doesn't weigh much: the train came and he let it pass, humbly and fully confident that it would pass by again at midday tomorrow.

This time the square he crossed on his way home was a white die open on top, it collected the booming tone of the bells in the church tower. Twelve, Anatol thought, and prepared to keep counting. But this stroke of the bells remained solitary, it fell into the middle of the square, was tossed high into the air by a motorcycle roaring through, and was scattered into the next street where it disappeared in a cloud of car exhaust. A mixed silence was all that remained. Anatol sighed: if you are expecting twelve, then one is rather meager. He would have found it more merciful if time were to descend back from its midday heights step by step, eleven strokes, ten, then nine . . . until six, and then back in the original direction, seven, eight . . . Then, instead of twelve hours, there would only have to be six, from one to six and back again to one. Every day would consist of two days, life would suddenly be twice as long, and we would never again hear the stroke of midnight, the hour of the spirits would be dropped, the army of ghosts would remain in a continual state of preparedness, lying in wait for the stroke of twelve, its cue, lying in wait—in vain.

After he had turned the lettuce over to Mrs. Mayer and was back in his room, he felt so miserable that he undressed and lay down on his bed. As soon as he closed his eyes the room was transformed into a turret along whose walls he felt in vain for doors that had been there when he came in. In order to escape from this prison he stared desperately at the ceiling, and a particle soon appeared drafting red and blue circles. He, Anatol, bringing death. The day begins with a premonition, and see here—someone else dies! His last day is never his last day: he always gives it away. The suicide victim on the bridge who changes his mind at the last moment, playing a trick on the river, taking back the existence he had just promised to give away, in place of this, however—out of some sense of propriety, most likely, although this is not easy to see—he accidentally gives someone standing near him a little shove: a tribute to the waves, a man keeps his word and now he can go on with his life, unperturbed, the whirlpools have stopped snapping at him . . .

But that's not right; he didn't give anyone a shove, that other person slipped; he had only been standing nearby and was surprised that he suddenly no longer had any desire to die. That's not really the way it happened, either. You don't just slip, not like that.

As an experiment Anatol tried closing his eyes, but opened them again when he found that his turret still had no doors. He was now seriously concerned. What should he do if it happened again? Don't get up, he said to himself, spare mankind his fatal presence . . . And if that didn't help? The telephone next to his bed rang and even as he was picking up the receiver he felt death leaving him, all he has to do is wait to hear the name of the person on the other end of the line about whose life he'll hear a report, quite surprising, he hears . . . Or Mrs. Mayer at the door: "There is a girl at the door, shall I let her in?" The girl is an old colleague, she was just passing by and thought he might be interested to know that just now, completely unexpected . . . He observes how vivacious she is, she is exhibiting the questionable cheerfulness of those still alive, who have just understood that they are still alive. "Simply gone," she says, "can you imagine? This morning dead in bed." And she asks him if *he* is sick, because he's still in bed at this hour . . . "I *was* sick," says Anatol, and is embarrassed by the simple truth, "but I feel a lot better now."

Another time it's a delivery boy with a telegram. The sound

of the doorbell crawls down Anatol's spine to his tailbone and continues ringing there on its own. At the same time the skin on his head tightens, making his hair stand up on its roots. It is just a notification that his ninety-year-old great-uncle, who outlived his own issue, had died and left his estate to Anatol. Anatol declines the opportunity to profit from his unhappy position and refuses the inheritance, a decision his lawyer applauds: "You have made the right choice. It would have cost you more in taxes than it's worth . . . "

Anatol cannot tolerate this state any longer; he is a fugitive, a man who hardly dares to open his eyes in the morning: another day of death? Or finally not? Death, which he has been approaching so full of trust, has defeated him in an indirect way, making him the hangman. Anatol has become allergic to everything related to death: he avoids cemeteries, even flower shops, gives away his black suit and wants nothing to do with those left behind, which condemns him to complete isolation once he comes to understand that the whole of mankind consists of those left behind.

An attempt to sneak away fails: barely has he reached the roof of the high-rise before he sees the tumult, hears the screams—someone else got there before him. Anatol spins around on his heels, retreats, and pushes the elevator button, which suddenly glows under the tip of his finger, as red and round as the rising sun over a black arrow pointing down.

The police officer he finally surrenders to on a dusty forenoon in a district office, between the wastepaper basket, cuspidor, and coat rack, laughs in his face. He laughs as loud as his uniform and as long as his breath will allow; then he becomes officious and wary, watching Anatol out of the corner of his eye while leafing through his most-wanted list; he convinces himself that Anatol cannot possibly be a suspect in any of the as yet unsolved murders, laughs again, but more sedately, and refers Anatol to a psychiatric hospital.

No one laughs here; the psychiatrist is amazed at nothing, the tricks of the human apparatus have long since ceased to fascinate him, he tosses his knowledge and his prescriptions into a bottomless pit; it is not his responsibility, it is his alibi. Anatol learns new words like *hypermnesia* and sees the world order tottering: people don't actually die because Anatol has sensed death in the morning, but on the contrary Anatol senses death in the morning because shortly thereafter someone will die. "Life is not a one-way street," says the psychiatrist, "is it?"

Anatol is cured of his premonitions as well as his belief in the order of things; he knows that anything is possible, causality from both directions, there he stands, defenseless. There is no safe point in time.

His mornings, however, have become harmless, no day seems to him to be the last and even the last day won't appear to him as such. And if he is suffering in deadly misery, then it is only because of strawberry punch: he would give his life for a glass, but his system can't take it.

We are disappointed in Vladimir. The big picture has completely passed him by except for a very minor inspiration; he has, says Cyril, made a molehill out of a mountain. "The things you keep demanding!" says Dombrowskaya. "How should a person find significance in death when he doesn't even take life seriously?"

Vladimir shows us a play, we see an audience attending a premiere, bejeweled ladies, smiling gentlemen, and in the first row our guests from the press. Now the curtain is going up and the audience is applauding. Onstage we see a lectern, a grand piano, chairs that start out empty but are soon occupied by people entering from the wings, both right and left.

There has been no effort made at all to make the set look real, a cabinet that opens exposing walls made of paper, the cellophane chandelier undulates in the wind, the tin piano responds to every touch with a hollow resonance. A cardboard tree next to the door has apparently been forgotten; it is showing its profile to the audience and is only some millimeters thick.

The actors are passionless, they're probably just extras who only care about finding a good seat. The front rows are immediately occupied, but some hardheads bring their own chairs and encircle the lectern and the grand piano. This all takes time: the premiere audience is becoming restless, isolated whistles can be heard from the balconies, in the background someone is yelling, "When you gonna get this thing under way?"

Finally everyone is seated, the people in the back rows have resigned themselves, some are still scraping the floor with their chairs, while those sitting in better seats have crossed their legs and folded their hands; they are all staring straight ahead full of expectation. A small piece of plaster drops from the slapdash construct of a stage-set ceiling onto the piano; whether this has happened by accident or according to the director's instruction remains unclear. It produces a thin, somehow pathetic tone, characteristic of the elements involved, plaster and tin.

At this moment the curtain falls. The audience is quiet, perplexed, but no one complains. A blond in the first row, probably a critic, stands up and says: "Well, that's it." Hundreds of others are mumbling, "That's it?" They leave.

"Well, that's it," says Vladimir as he switches off the projector. He's tricked us again, we're all a little peeved. Only Penny is stupid enough to ask him why the plaster fell from the ceiling. Vladimir, we knew before she asked, hasn't got a clue.

"Why does plaster fall from the ceiling? Maybe because the ceiling was badly painted, or it's old. You should really ask the set designers." It is true, he really doesn't know; we laugh.

Nadine can't stand Anatol; she calls him morbid, degenerate, incapable of living a life. She says it's really asking too much to be expected to live with such a being in one house and that she's completely fed up. All the while she's looking around, challenging us, but if one of us makes the mistake of opening his mouth, she interrupts immediately:

"Yes, yes, I know. I'm doing him an injustice. He is an angel. A gentle person of great intelligence. Sensitive, he really is, as shy as a daisy. His ear, like the ear of a bat, detects tones that are lost to us, he is like the branch of a weeping willow blowing in the wind, a mobile! So delicate, so vulnerable! We know he outdoes the flora and fauna when it comes to sensibilities. He has," she says, struggling for breath, "every prerequisite necessary to ruin us."

Her new encounter has just made things worse; she feels threatened.

"If it were not for *him*, then you wouldn't be such cowards!"

"There is something to that," says Dombrowskaya. "We must show him some consideration; he does live here after all." Nadine begins to cry and the mood turns rather unpleasant. Anatol has not taken part in this discussion. He is standing at the window; what he sees is: a street that empties into a square which can no longer be seen. The houses are sketched in, black edges shaded gray, the windows are thicker strokes, everything brightens toward the top. A lot of rock, very little sky, chimneys and antennas on the rooftops where a half-moon is crawling around, its end is Anatol's future, the next day.

Nadine causes Anatol no less suffering. The mornings he awakes so vulnerable, unprotected, exposed to the dangers of the new day, plotting ways to survive them—and on which he is suddenly confronted with Nadine: her house slippers hammer on his skull whenever she steps off the carpet, and the sound of her voice makes martyrs of his ears, Anatol hears her in syncopation as if through curtains of atmospheric disturbance, part weather report, part twelve-tone composition. Nadine is in a good mood but Anatol is moaning.

Vladimir has had another inspiration after all, he is playing a carnival barker:

"Well, well, ladies and gentlemen, you're reluctant to come a little closer, you're reluctant to come into my tent? On my honor, ladies and gentlemen, that will be your loss! You are not yet acquainted with the New Death. You only know that bag of bones with the scythe, a relic of the Middle Ages. Ladies and gentlemen, I assure you the Middle Ages have just come to an end! Gone the reaper with his blade, the boatman who carried you away in a skiff over dark waters— the New Death makes his appearance in a different way: he races in, horns honking, brakes squealing, and once you've been bagged, he puts you aboard a spaceship and there you float, not sitting, not lying down, rid of gravity once and for all . . . You lose your sense of time, sense of space, sense of fear . . . every possible sense, lost . . . You are finally free, you hurtle through light-years of space along precisely calculated paths, though light-years and distances in space are no longer of any concern to you, you hurtle—and you land! Whether you believe it or not, ladies and gentlemen—you land! Where, you ask? Where is not important, your affinities decide, only that which is related attracts, the selection is enormous, look around you, look up: the night is full of landing sites . . . One single look with open eyes and you will have stopped clinging to this underdeveloped star . . . Even this tiny tip of the Milky Way which you can observe, which in turn represents only a tiny fraction of existing galaxies—even on this tiny tip you can find thousands of better choices, what am I saying—thousands and thousands of thousands (small numbers, just one more of this planet's shortcomings . . .). Come on in, ladies and gentlemen, you will presently have the grand multiplication table at your fingertips . . . For the stars in the heavens are your past and your future: You will land among new beings who will accept you immediately, for scarcely will you have entered the atmosphere of their star before you are one of them, and none will ask from where you have come. You will have forgotten the earth, no loss to you, you're already enjoying a better life . . . They will bring you bangles and silver spoons and give you a name, or two, or three . . . On my honor ladies and gentlemen, you will have no regrets . . . "

Cyril is being contentious again in the way he speaks: "So-what, so-what, so-what-if, so-whatever-may-be-anyway," and it's getting on our nerves; he does it to get a rise out of Vladimir, but it never works; the only thing that gets a rise out of Vladimir is an inspiration—"for an inspiration," says Cyril, "he would sell our own grandmother," convincing no one, it's only a sign of Cyril's ill will. But Cyril won't let go, it's gnawing at him, so he takes another tack: "Distance, that's Vladimir's whole secret," he says, "and he would not have been able to keep it if he had ever gotten close to any living being or any single thing. But he hasn't, not even to us. He couldn't care less. Whether Anatol intends to do away with us or Sandra gives us up to the jungle, Vladimir is unmoved, he sits there and waits for an inspiration."

Nadine can't help herself; given her involvement with clothes, shoes, skin, and hair, she is left exposed to the mercies of an external life unless she can be satisfied with the flattery in her innermost circle, so to speak, and she can't.

Now, and this doesn't surprise us, she is sitting at her dressing table inspecting her appearance (the unavoidable consequence of a new conquest), and, at the same time, starting a fight with us (the consequence of every such inspection).

"This endless self-reflection," she says, and she's not referring to herself but to our conversations. "I just detest it. Sterile, that's what it is, sterile." How should we respond? We let her talk. She has just found a tiny, but apparently new, wrinkle on her forehead, a circumstance she finds utterly infuriating.

"How did I ever get wrinkles on my forehead?" she asks with some justification. "They certainly aren't mine!" She glares at us accusingly, but no one wants to take responsibility for this new wrinkle. "It is a crying shame: one single face for an entire house full of people! People who smoke" (this is meant for Anatol and Dombrowskaya), "people who think and spend their nights huddled over books . . . " (for the most part Cyril), "who make ugly faces" (this means Penny), "and can only be gotten out of the house with the greatest of difficulty" (meaning all of us). "How is a person to keep looking young?" asks Nadine. "No chance around here."

Cyril feels the need to protest. He finds Nadine's preoccupation with youth to be downright grotesque. For the ancient Chinese, he tells us, it was an insult to be considered young because that meant inexperienced, immature, green . . .

"That will be a great consolation to me if ever I meet up with an ancient Chinese," says Nadine.

At first Dombrowskaya keeps out of the fight; her opinion is well known: Why? she asks, would I ever spend four-fifths of my time trying to gain time, and then spend four-fifths of that time trying to gain more time? I am no mathematician, she says, but it just doesn't appear to be worth it . . . Charm, she says, is much more important.

For whatever charm we have we are beholden to Kay, or, even more so, to her homeliness: not one of us, not even Nadine, will ever rely completely on their outward appearance as long as we have this creature in our house; we find her extremely unattractive: dark, pensive, biting her nails, while searching for a common thread running through the chaos of her potential . . . We respect this characteristic, it is a constant reminder to us to apply ourselves. It is our imminent homeliness that makes us content. No compliment was ever wasted on us: we think of Kay, we are amazed and grateful.

But Nadine, sitting in front of the mirror, deciphers and

curses the signs of time. She wants to be beautiful for this new man—"Dombrowskaya is more beautiful than you are," says Cyril—she wants to be young for him—"Youth," he says, "is no advantage." All this is true, but she's not listening.

Only Penny stands by Nadine, even encouraging her in her vanity:

"You have to become much, much more beautiful, until you are as beautiful as my lady!" By *my lady* Penny means her own drawing of a person who possesses every possible attribute of beauty as seen through Penny's eyes: wasplike waist, a forest of lashes, a mouth like a lobster . . . No one knows where she collected these impressions, we only know that she has more of these pictures and that she never hesitates to tyrannize us with them.

This used to be her favorite gag: whenever a new person appeared in our house, Penny would pull a crumpled piece of paper covered with smears of colored pencil out of her school bag and shove it under the nose of our newcomer. The poor newcomer couldn't avoid seeing her own caricature in those scribbles, insulting and distorted though they were.

For a while we tried to defend ourselves.

"A grotesque state of affairs," said Cyril. "You'd almost think she'd created us."

Talk like this only encouraged Penny. She took out another stack of portraits and waved them like a fan in our faces. A fleeting reflection that caused us to blush. Then she snapped the fan shut and swatted her school bag.

"I've got more in here," she said.

"And what if you do." We were determined to conceal our curiosity. To acknowledge Penny is to admit defeat.

The only exception was Sandra's arrival. Her picture was not among Penny's collection. We saw the little one sitting on the floor pawing ever more vigorously through the contents of her bag. She removed each piece of paper, one by one, inspected both sides before putting it back. From time to time she glared up at Sandra suspiciously, as if she saw in her a mistake that might be cleared up at any moment. Sandra didn't even take notice of her.

It was Dombrowskaya who finally put an end to this picture stunt; she stood on the bottom step of the stairway and shouted into the gloomy room:

"My God! Some progress we've made, haven't we!"

Someone jumped up and turned on a lamp, and thus illuminated we could see each other's sad and tearstained faces; Nadine took out her compact and began quickly powdering her nose, Cyril was flustered and coughed, and Anatol smiled. Dombrowskaya was studying one of Penny's works in which she appeared as an imposing lady with a hat, necklace, long gloves, and an overly long cigarette holder.

"That's right," she said, "the cigarette holder! I'll have to get one. Aside from that, I always play by the rules, as you can see." Penny was triumphant. Dombrowskaya was the first among us to recognize her beginnings in this depraved child.

There was no time for explanations: Dombrowskaya went out to the Regina for lunch. This is just another of her obligations. She sat upright in the taxi and took the city's measure. In houses and stores, in the layout of the streets, she saw the scarcely concealed products of childish fantasies, on the monuments stood people who had promised themselves when they were ten years old that they would end up on a monument—a thought that showed the fragmentation in Penny's world of pictures: a child who can be distracted, possessed of one dream today and another tomorrow . . . There would be no monument in Penny's future.

Dombrowskaya amused herself; driving on, she saw accomplishments that were nothing more than reproductions of accomplishments of which callow boys and girls had dreamed decades ago: libraries, museums, Cleopatra's supersized brow gracing a movie poster, even the bank robbers on the kiosk—nothing but children's dreams fulfilled.

Lunch was delightful. She looked down the table: behind

each chair stood a grinning schoolchild admiring his work. All of them were in gym wear, striped yachting shirts that were popular thirty years ago, hair properly parted, jug-eared with impudent tongues: Dombrowskaya recognized the handball team of a coed grammar school whose picture had been taken while they were standing in the schoolyard under the sign *The Victors*.

The pride at this table was founded on more than a simple handball victory; they had also won the track meet, at least up to this round, and they weren't about to slack off. Their goals were firm, their powers knew no bounds, their self-assurance seemed prodigious.

At the foot of the table an elderly gentleman talked about the export curve of his company; between numbers and trends, names flashed through: Bombay, San Francisco, Rio de Janeiro . . . They were nothing but names in his report, but there was triumph on the face of the boy standing behind his chair, a triumph that engendered admiration and envy among the entire team, especially among the boys. For a few minutes even Penny surrendered herself to her oldest yearning: to shrink the earth. With each city visited, each coast traveled, it would become a little smaller until it could be turned like a globe, then held in two hands, and finally, once it had been entirely explored, put into her pocket. And then? Penny turned away as the export manager put down his fork and reached into the pocket of his dark suit, looking for the missing earth among his keys and cigar cutter.

The man sitting next to Dombrowskaya talked about a colleague who was currently being treated in a sanatorium: "He didn't simply work too hard, but what's more important, he worked too well: the machine was so well-oiled that it ran without him. He made himself superfluous. As soon as he understood this, he fell ill, and then he really understood what had happened. . . That's why he won't get well again, either. The only thing that could bring him back to health would be a full-fledged breakdown in his shop so he could see that he was needed again. But tell that to the supervisor . . . " Hearing this the young boys stopped grinning and, full of contempt, let the corners of their mouths droop; they didn't accept defeatists of this ilk. This was someone who had reached his goal, and, unable to apply the brakes, had shot past it into the abyss . . . One of the group had even gone so far as to tap his temple with his index finger. Fortunately, dessert was now being served. In her fruit salad, spiced with maraschino, Dombrowskaya recognized the pattern of a world that owed, in equal measure, both its security and its narrow-mindedness to the aspirations of a teenage handball team.

Vladimir thoroughly enjoyed this evening: first he played the rascal for us, dressed in a red and white striped polo shirt and giving a speech at a banquet. We saw the elegantly appointed table, chests draped in smoking jackets, and chinchilla collars.

"Ladies and gentlemen!" (Even the sonorous organ was practiced, Vladimir has always managed to improve upon nature where necessary.) "By the time I reached the age of ten, I had already decided to become rich, very, very rich . . . You ask why? No, you don't ask, but I'll tell you anyway: because I wanted to have things that could be bought with money . . . " (applause), "things like power, elegance, a happy disposition . . . " (louder applause), " . . . not to mention all the usual trivialities. Ladies and gentlemen, may I tell you, in all modesty: I have succeeded." (At this point we hear the first cheers.) "And furthermore, may I say, it was not given to me. You all know about the rocky road to success, the days of bitter toil, nights darkened by the volatility of the exchange rate—no effort was too great, no means too insignificant, and all of this to fulfill a promise I made to myself at the tender age of ten years . . . " (here a few words are swallowed up in the applause). "And thus, ladies and gentlemen, I can no longer withhold from you my secret: that at the age of ten I was just as smart as I am today!" (Cheers and applause, a monocle shouts *bravissimo!*, a fifteen-carat diamond necklace throws him a rose, he sits down.)

Penny laughed the loudest; she didn't feel that any of this had been meant for her and told everyone within range that little boys were silly. But this performance had a second act, and now it was clearly Penny who, dressed in a white uniform with high boots, was standing in the center ring with her whip. The supporting actor, a tiger, reminded us of Sandra at first, then immediately of everyone else, Dombrowskaya, Anatol, Nadine, Cyril, Bozena—least of all a tiger. This tiger wears its coat like a pair of baggy pajamas, loose at the neck, accordion folds at the legs; still it lopes around quite gracefully on all fours.

Now Penny is carrying a stool to the middle of the cage, cracking her whip and yelling, "Alley-oop!" The tiger jumps. Penny gets another stool, puts it on top of the first one, yells, "Alley-oop!" and cracks her whip. The tiger jumps over this obstacle, but because of its loose skin brushes a stool with one paw.

"Good tiger," says Penny. The tiger growls. The little one has gone to get a hoop wrapped in a piece of gasoline-soaked felt. She walks up with a pretty smile, the tiger spits and paws at her, but the crack of her whip brings him into a cowering crouch. Penny looks him in the eye, the tiger gathers himself for a leap. Penny yells "Hup!" at the same moment the hoop bursts into flames. Propelled by something between fear and force, the tiger emerges from the fire. Penny shouts "Bravo!," throws the hoop away, and bows to the bleachers all around; the bleachers are empty, this animal act is closed to the public. While she is still in her bow, the tiger leaps on his tormentor from behind, throws her down to the ground, and swallows her whole. No one comes to her rescue.

Later the tiger is lying alone in his cage, licking its paws and pondering the question of who is more dangerous for whom, the trainer for the tiger or the tiger for the trainer. "We need to define the term danger." Penny would have known. "If only she were to be brought back, we could clarify things." Penny, from the belly of the tiger, says: "Not again."

Nadine is putting on her coat. We are watching her very closely. She takes her coat from the hanger, puts the hanger back, slips into the right arm, slips into the left, reaches into her pockets to make sure that everything is there, pushes her sleeves up, because that gives her greater freedom of movement, and then pulls the two halves of the coat together snugly, one over the other for protection: from him or from us, it is hard to say.

She is ready to go out. So as to allow for no doubts about the finality of her decision, she seats herself like a visitor on the edge of a chair, sets her purse down next to her, and plays with her gloves, alternately stretching and then hitting her knee with them; we can see by this that she is still afraid of us.

We are no longer even attempting to hold her back. We have done our best. We have spread out before her all of the useful knowledge at our command; she has not heeded our warnings.

"I would have been surprised if she had," says Dombrowskaya, surveying her solitaire hand. "It was one of our earliest experiences that we learn nothing from experience, an experience we confirm over and over again by not learning from it."

"Adages," says Cyril. "Nice, but whom are they going to help? I can't use them in my work." For a moment he lets himself be overwhelmed again by his worries: "Heaven help us, what a story this will be! Just thinking of Stranitzky . . . I can see his face reading: as if he had just bit on a decayed tooth, an exposed nerve; it hurts that much."

"Just think," says Vladimir, "of this man with the decayed tooth as one of the many Stranitzkys, and not even the most intelligent one, at that . . . "

"I am thinking about it," says Cyril, "but what good will it do me, unless Stranitzky thinks about it too . . . "

"Stop this," says Dombrowskaya, "I can't hear that name anymore." And so we leave Stranitzky behind, if only for the moment, but still . . .

Nadine, perched on the edge of her chair, commands a view of most of the street. It is the same street she walked down this afternoon with a spring in her step, but now it is artificially illuminated, neon lights on quicksilver puddles. Nadine believes that this is the only difference. She gathers herself, that is, she gathers us, that is, we are all looking out of the window, even Anatol, even Kay. Penny alone is sitting on the carpet digging through her school bag.

"Don't bother," says Dombrowskaya, "the new one arriving now hasn't come from your collection."

The new one? The word lands like a fist. As familiar as we are with this possibility, its actual realization, which appears to be imminent, causes us some anxiety. What will she be like? What will she undertake? Will she sell us out to this new man? We look for Anatol: if there is any reason to be afraid, then he'll be the first to show us where the danger lies. But Anatol is so calm that he surprises himself.

"Funny," he says, "I'm not afraid at all; I can't help it, it's almost as if I were looking forward to this."

"Frightening," says Cyril, and Vladimir, not able to resist an inspiration, proclaims Anatol's wisdom:

"His hopes have not been realized, giving him reason to hope that his fears won't be realized, either . . . that shows a true talent for living! Take this example to heart, children!" His cheerfulness is contagious; this moment in history is already threatening to dissolve into merriment when we hear Nadine exclaim.

We know this sound, it is a call welcoming the wondrous, which is also the dangerous, always. The new man has come into view, dimly for most of us, nothing but a shadow under neon light. Something is going happen, many things are possible.

"I just wish—," begins Bozena.

"Me too," says Sandra, "but something entirely different."

"Quiet," says Dombrowskaya. At this moment Nadine gets up, takes off her coat, and carries it out into the hallway. When she returns we see that she has a surprise for us.

"Ha," she says, "if you only knew!"

"If you mean the newcomer," says Cyril, pointing toward the hallway with his head, "you can spare yourself the exaggeration. She is after all just one of us, and the prerequisites," he looks around, "are understood only too well."

"Still," says Nadine.

We can now hear steps outside the door and a quiet cough.

"Hardly shown up and already chilled," says Vladimir.

"Better be thinking of a name for her," says Cyril, and Penny, who would like to detract attention from the gap in her supply of pictures, shouts:

"I've got one!"

"We're in no hurry with this name business," says Dombrowskaya. "The important thing now is for her to take over the next steps for us." The next steps: those are the steps she will take with the new man.

"I'm sure she'll be happy to," says Nadine.

We don't doubt it. Thus, in a minute or so, she will put on Nadine's coat and hat, open the door with the post horn handle, and go out into the street to the stranger, nonchalantly, unperturbed. The doorbell has only to ring.